3 BRIDES
for
3 BAD BOYS

3 BRIDES
for
3 BAD BOYS

LUCY MONROE

BRAVA

KENSINGTON PUBLISHING CORP.

BRAVA BOOKS are published by

Kensington Publishing Corp.
850 Third Avenue
New York, NY 10022

ISBN 0-7394-5042-5

Printed in the United States of America

To my aunts, Lois, Marge and Nita.
I love you each of you
for very special reasons.
Blessings,
Lucy

Contents

A Deal Is a Deal

Chapter One

Rand Alexander should have a warning sign.

Danger.

Radioactive material.

Beware.

Because he impacted Phoebe's senses like a nuclear power plant going into meltdown.

She sucked in air, trying to regulate breathing that had gone haywire the moment his to-die-for body had filled the doorway of the swank hotel's reception room.

Heart racing, she fought the painful intensity of desires that would shock Rand silly. *Like she always did.* Every time the man walked into the room, she lost control of her body's reactions.

And he didn't even notice.

It wasn't that he ignored her. They were friends, after all, but if she danced naked on the hood of his car, he would politely ask her if she needed a hand down. All the while his real focus would be on something, or someone, else.

Like the blonde whose dress looked as if it was made of shimmering silver spangles glued to her body. The one that had just caught his arm and his attention.

"He looks wonderful, doesn't he, Phoebe dear? So mature

now." Aunt Emmaline's voice buzzed at the edge of Phoebe's consciousness like a bee trying to alight.

Wonderful? He looked edible, six feet four inches of solid sex appeal with glossy black hair and eyes the color of molten steel.

"Fancy him coming back after all these years and still unattached."

Of course he was unattached. He had buried his heart with his wife and son six years ago.

"Oh, look, he and his mother are coming this way."

It was only as her aunt's last words registered that Phoebe realized the old woman was not discussing Rand, but rather his half brother, Carter Sloane. Her ex-fiancé.

While Rand turned aside to talk to the blonde, Carter was indeed headed their way. Walking beside his elegant mother, he looked more like a California golden boy than an East Coast executive.

"Carter, how well you look." Aunt Emmaline beamed at him.

"Thank you, and may I return the compliment?"

The old woman's paper-thin cheeks pinkened under the warmth of Carter's smile. It was the same smile that four years ago had made Phoebe's heart race, but it did not have the slightest impact now. Rand, on the other hand, only had to look at her and her brain stopped working.

The older women greeted each other.

"Phoebe, how are you?" Carter's attention was fixed wholly on her now, and she tried to return the favor.

Only Rand and the other woman were laughing together, and the sight of red fingernails against a white dinner jacket had Phoebe fighting green demons she hated almost as much as her status as a twenty-five-year-old virgin.

"I'm fine, Carter." She forced her eyes away from the couple on the other side of the room. "It's been a long time."

"Yes, it has."

"How long will you be staying?"

He shrugged. "I may be back for good."

His mother looked unmoved by the prospect, but not so Aunt Emmaline. "How wonderful!" She smiled with a definite gleam in her eye. "You and Phoebe will have to catch up on old times."

A sinking feeling in the pit of her stomach told Phoebe she had to divert this conversational tangent but fast. "The past is over, and I'm sure Carter has no more interest in it than I do."

Aunt Emmaline frowned. "You don't mean that, dear."

"I do." Phoebe smiled at Carter to show no offense was intended by her blunt declaration, but blunt was all that worked with her great-aunt.

"Standing on four-year-old pride makes for a lonely existence." The acerbity of her aunt's tone didn't bother Phoebe nearly as much as the implication she'd spent four years pining for a man who'd dumped her.

"I'm not being proud, just practical. It's only fair to tell you that if you're considering Carter as a candidate for great-nephew-in-law, then don't bother. We've been there, done that, and it didn't work. Right, Carter?"

She turned to Carter and willed him to agree with her.

His expression was regretful, but he remained quiet, which did nothing to help the situation or settle her temper.

"I suppose you think Rand Alexander is a better prospect?" Aunt Emmaline demanded, warming to an old argument. She glared in disapproval toward the couple on the other side of the ballroom, now blatantly flirting.

"That could hardly be the case." Mrs. Sloane's well-bred sneer grated on Phoebe's nerves.

She had her reasons for resenting Rand, but Phoebe would not stand silently by while she and Aunt Emmaline criticized him.

"You're interested in my half brother?" The incredulity in

Carter's voice was almost enough for her to answer in the affirmative, putting her feelings for Rand on public display.

Almost, but her pride was still stronger than her indignation, so she remained silent and let Carter draw his own conclusions.

"He's not really your type, Phoebe." Carter sounded as though he almost pitied her.

And that hurt because although he was dead wrong that his half brother wasn't *her* type, there was no denying she wasn't in a league to entice Rand, and that amounted to the same depressing thing.

Aunt Emmaline bristled as only very correct old ladies could do. "Of course he's not."

Phoebe turned on her aunt. "What's wrong with Rand?"

A tinkling laugh sounded from the other side of the room, snagging her attention in time to see the blonde rub up against Rand like a horny cat, eroding Phoebe's temper one more notch.

"He's unsuitable."

"That's ridiculous. He's an incredible man. His charitable contributions last year were twice that of any other businessman in New Hope. You know he is one of tonight's major supporters."

Aunt Emmaline went to speak, but Phoebe plowed on, her fury overcoming her good sense. "He's only thirty years old and the business he started without any help from his *family* is already a Fortune 500 company. His father may have been an unfaithful rat, but Rand never even flirted with another woman during his marriage."

Her hand flew to her mouth. She hadn't meant to say that, and she belatedly looked at Carter and his mother to see how they'd taken her reference to Hoyt Sloane. Carter's expression looked carved from granite, and his mother was doing her best to pretend not to have heard. Filled with remorse, Phoebe opened her mouth to apologize.

"He may have been faithful during his marriage," Aunt Emmaline said, forestalling the apology and completely ignoring Phoebe's reference to Rand and Carter's father, "but he's certainly made up for it since his wife's death. The man's a womanizer, plain and simple."

"Rand is not a womanizer!" Phoebe slotted in.

"Sweetheart, you've got to admit that you're not up to Rand's speed." Carter's tone was conciliatory, but Phoebe didn't feel like being soothed.

"And why would she want to be?" Mrs. Sloane asked.

Regret for her hasty words dissolved, and Phoebe's slow burn rose to a boil.

"My niece can do much better," Aunt Emmaline added with a significant look at Carter.

The thread holding Phoebe's temper in check snapped.

"I'd give up my trust fund to have Rand Alexander notice I'm female." Ignoring the inner voice that warned her to stop while she was ahead, she added, "And I'd give everything I own for just one week in his bed."

Aunt Emmaline's lips moved, her mouth opening and closing, but no sound came out. Her eyes focused over Phoebe's shoulder, and she waved her hand in front of her face like a fan. Carter looked like he'd swallowed a fish whole. Mrs. Sloane's lips pursed as if she'd just sucked on a lemon, but they remained closed. Good. That had finally shut them up.

"I know you're female."

She heard the voice, and everything inside her rebelled at the knowledge of who it belonged to. But even if the sexy timbre wasn't undeniably familiar, she could not mistake the *feel* of Rand's presence.

It took all of her courage to turn around and face him. He was alone. Relief whooshed through her. It was bad enough that he had heard her, but to have the spangle-clad blonde privy to Phoebe's stupidity would have been the limit.

She went hot, then cold with embarrassment as she forced herself to meet his eyes. "Good evening, Rand."

He didn't so much as crack a social smile. "I don't need the inducement of your trust fund to recognize you are a woman." Another man would have pretended not to hear, but Rand lived by his own rules, and none of them included polite social lies.

"Of course not. I mean, it's obvious I'm not male." Then mentally considering her curves that could better be described as bumps, she amended, "Fairly obvious anyway."

He raised his brow, his gaze sweeping over her with tactile intensity. Things happened to her insides that had no business happening in the current situation.

He took her wrist in his hand. "Are you ready to go?"

The feel of his skin against hers had her staring at him stupidly. For all the time they'd spent together since Carter's desertion, he'd never touched her before. "What?"

"You said you'd give everything you own for a week in my bed. I'll settle for the deed to Luna Island."

Chapter Two

"Now, wait just a damned minute." Carter's protest barely registered with Phoebe.

A week in Rand's bed?

"Are you coming?" Rand asked, his eyes cold, metallic silver.

But his thumb rubbed the inside of her wrist, and a totally inappropriate answer to his question came to mind. She wanted to come. Only not the kind of coming he was talking about and only with him.

Her silence didn't phase him, and he started tugging her toward the exit.

Her aunt made a squawking sound, and Carter said something to Rand that he ignored.

Suddenly, Carter's hand clamped down around her other wrist. His hold was not nearly as gentle as Rand's, and it pulled her to an abrupt halt. Rand stopped and turned. His eyes seared Carter, and she was really glad that look wasn't directed at her.

"Let her go."

"No." Carter looked pretty intimidating himself. "You aren't going to take advantage of her feelings for you to get the island."

"Isn't that what you planned to do, or are you going to try to convince me you came back at this particular point in time to renew family ties?"

She didn't understand what Rand was talking about, but no one could miss the frozen scorn in his voice.

"My reasons for coming back aren't the issue here."

"They are if they include trading on old feelings to talk Phoebe out of Luna Island."

"*I'm* not going to hurt her."

"Neither am I."

They were like two stags facing each other, their stances battle ready, and she was in the middle. It was such a novel sensation that she didn't immediately object to being discussed as if she wasn't there.

"Like hell." Carter pulled her toward him, and pain shot up into her shoulder.

"Stop that right now. You're hurting me!"

Carter's hold loosened immediately, but he didn't let go, and neither did Rand. They glowered at each other, making the very air around them crackle with tension.

"What's going on?"

Rand looked away from his brother to meet her gaze. "I'll explain it when we're alone."

"You're not taking her anywhere, damn it."

She broke eye contact with Rand and fixed her gaze on Carter. This man had broken their engagement with no more explanation than that it wasn't the right time to get married. He had left her to face public humiliation four years ago while he traveled the world, experiencing things she only dreamed of.

His concern was years too late.

"Let me go."

"You're setting yourself up for a fall." He looked like he really cared. "He just wants to use you."

"That's not your problem." She tugged at her arm.

Carter shook his head, but released her. "Don't let him do this to you, Phoebe. He wants the deed to the island. That's all."

The one thing he could not possibly comprehend was that she wanted Rand to do things to her. Wild things. Wicked things. And if it meant giving up the deed to an island she had never even visited, she was more than willing to do so.

Rand started walking again, and she let him pull her along. She wasn't worried about her aunt following. Causing a scene was anathema to her, though Phoebe had no doubt Carter would bear the brunt of Aunt Emmaline's displeasure for letting her leave with Rand. She had no idea what Mrs. Sloane would say and didn't care.

They made it all the way to the car park of the hotel without her pseudokidnapper saying a word.

"Rand!"

He stopped and turned to look at her, his expression strangely dispassionate. "What?"

"Where are you taking me?"

"To my bed."

Rand watched as Phoebe's perfect oval face blanched of color. "That *is* what you said you wanted."

He didn't know why he was pushing her like this. He had no intention of taking her to bed, but something inexplicable had invaded his psyche when he saw Carter make a beeline for her and her great-aunt the minute he arrived at the charity reception.

Rand had been sure in that instant that his brother was aware of the satellite scan and what it had shown on Luna Island.

Carter had been running Sloane Electronics from the Manhattan office since their father's death. He had not returned even once to their small Massachusetts town after breaking his engagement with Phoebe, but now he had a good reason for coming back, and it had nothing to do with wanting to renew a broken relationship.

The fact that he might use that old relationship to his advantage in securing the deed to Luna Island had provoked feelings in Rand that he didn't like. Didn't want.

Protective feelings he had thought died with his wife and son six years ago.

Emotions he *wanted* just as dead as his family.

He could accept being angry at the thought of Carter trying to seduce the land away from Phoebe because both men wanted what those satellite scans had shown, but the fury that had all but overwhelmed him at the thought of his half brother in bed with the shy beauty bothered him. He should not care.

She was his friend, but nothing more.

"What's the matter, Phoebe," he taunted, needing to make her pay for the feelings she evoked, "changed your mind?"

He expected her to agree and ask him to let her go. Something he wasn't entirely sure he could do and that made him angrier than his half brother's attempt to preempt him with Luna Island.

She didn't say anything, but he could feel the wild beat of her heart in the pulse under his fingers. Her skin was so smooth, so soft. His thumb glided over it, seeking the animal pleasure the small movement gave him. The idea of taking her to his bed was a hell of a lot more appealing than it should have been.

Since Susan's death, he had not wanted any particular woman, just physical release. And he'd taken it, with women sophisticated enough to know the score and accept the tally.

Phoebe was neither of those.

She was white roses, wedding registries and babies.

He shuddered at the thought. Never again.

Which was why he had ignored the way her eyes ate him

alive whenever they were together. It was why he ignored his own base reaction to her slender curves and his desire to touch silky hair that looked like warmed honey when she wore it down. It was why he cursed the dreams that were no longer haunted by his dead wife but a twenty-five-year-old virgin who he could not and would not have.

Angry with himself for his lack of mental control and furious with Phoebe for being the source of his sexual frustration, he tugged her to the passenger side of his silver Jaguar. Opening the door, he said, "Get in."

She didn't move.

"What's the problem?" His jaw clenched. He sounded like an angry lion; no wonder she flinched.

Then her chin tilted, and she straightened to her full height, which was a good ten inches shorter than his. "I'm trying to decide if I want to let you boss me around like this, or not."

He wanted to kiss that mutinous bow of a mouth, which was damned dangerous. "You do."

Even sweet Phoebe had her limits. Any second now, she was going to blast him with a pithy lecture on equality between the sexes and then stomp away. Which was exactly what he wanted.

To hell with what his sex was clamoring for. Going horizontal, hot and sweaty with Phoebe was not on the agenda. No way. No how.

Hazel eyes that should be shooting sparks of anger went dark with unmistakable sexual hunger. "Maybe I do at that."

He stood there, sucker-punched, while she got in the car, tucking the folds of her swirling skirt inside and pulling the door shut. Stunned disbelief and desire so strong it made his knees want to buckle held him immobile for several seconds before he circled the car and got in.

He turned to face her. Her hands were twisted together in her lap, and her face was averted. *So much for her sexual daring.* He dismissed the disappointment ripping at his insides as a normal reaction to having to go without sex when he wanted it more than he wanted that damn island.

He started the engine and pulled the powerful car out of its parking space. "Right. We need to talk."

There was no pretty way to package the truth, so he didn't even try. "Carter came back because he wants Luna Island. So do I."

"I got that much at the reception." She didn't sound real bothered by the fact. "But what I don't understand is why? I'd understand if you were land developers, but you're not. Your company is into computers, and Sloane Electronics makes televisions and things. What good would a Mexican island do either of you? Nobody even lives there."

"Satellite scans have revealed a large deposit of lithium."

She stared at him as if he were talking Swahili. "So?"

He found himself smiling. He liked the way she went directly to the point. In a society that thrived on socially acceptable dishonesty, Phoebe's straightforward attitude was more than refreshing. He'd realized in the past few years that it could be addictive.

"It's a mineral that is in short supply worldwide, and a deposit like this could bring down the cost of manufacturing lithium-based products significantly."

"But how could you *both* need it?"

"It's used in flat screen technology for both computer monitors and televisions."

"I see."

"Do you?"

"What do you mean?"

"You and Carter were engaged, but he didn't come back for you." It was important she understood that and didn't get taken in by his brother's charm.

"Contrary to my aunt's fond hopes, I didn't imagine for a minute that he had."

"You're bound to be vulnerable to him."

"Am I?"

He flicked a glance at her, but it revealed nothing.

"You were engaged once."

"That was a long time ago. Things change. People change."

"You haven't married. You hardly date. Everyone thinks you've been waiting for Carter to come back."

"I wouldn't have considered you the type to listen to gossip."

"It makes sense."

"I suppose it does." She adjusted her seat belt across her chest, pressing her delicate curves into prominence. "But whoever thinks I've been pining for Carter is wrong."

Her words registered, but so did the shape of her breasts. He had to make a fast correction to stop from driving off the road as need, sharp and urgent, arced through him.

"I'm glad to hear that." He didn't want her hurt by his brother a second time, but he wasn't sure he believed her.

She'd been devastated when Carter had left four years ago.

She fiddled with her skirt, smoothing it over her knees. "You said you'd give me a week in your bed in exchange for the deed, is that right?"

This time he narrowly missed going up on the sidewalk and swore. "I was being sarcastic. Your aunt and Carter's mother pissed me off. I wanted to shock the look of condescending disapproval right off their faces." The fact that he had wanted to get Phoebe away from Carter, he left unsaid. "I don't expect you to sleep with me. I'll pay fair price for the island and give you an ongoing percentage on the minerals mined."

He drove the Jag into the parking garage for his apartment building and pulled into his assigned spot. Turning off the ignition, he said, "We can go over the details upstairs. You'll probably want to have a geologist's survey done."

She didn't move. "A deal is a deal."

What deal?

No way could she seriously expect him to take her to bed. She'd just been spouting off, protecting him as she often did when she thought someone was criticizing him. It was an endearing trait if unnecessary.

He'd stopped worrying about what other people thought the year he learned his dad was married to a woman besides his mother and he had a half brother he'd never met.

"Come off it, honey. The joke has gone far enough. We need to talk business."

Her sweet lips firmed in a stubborn line. "I'm not joking."

"And I'm no stud for hire," he gritted out.

She looked completely unimpressed by that assurance. "Then I'll just have to offer the deal to Carter. He liked me well enough once to want to marry me; maybe he won't find it such a hardship to take me to bed."

Chapter Three

"Tell me you didn't just say that."

She shook her head, her face an interesting shade of red.

Phoebe Garrison, undeniably shy and almost certainly a virgin, had just threatened to offer her island in exchange for a week in his damned brother's bed if Rand didn't stick with the deal. He refused to believe it.

She was silent enough now. Sitting there with her legs crossed primly at the ankle under her silky skirt.

This whole discussion was crazy.

She had to be bluffing, but if she wasn't, his brother could bed Phoebe and have the papers on the mineral rights signed by morning.

Rand's teeth ground together.

He was not taking her to bed, but neither was Carter.

She'd better regain her sanity soon because he was close to losing his. He shoved his door open. "Come on."

She hadn't unbuckled her seat belt. "Where are we?"

"My apartment."

"What are we doing here?"

He rolled his eyes at the question asked in such a tiny voice. One minute she was demanding he pay for Luna Island with his sexual expertise; the next she was acting like a frightened maiden from a medieval fantasy.

"It's where I keep my bed," he said to punish her for tempting him with something he could not have, even as he felt relief that her insanity appeared to be ebbing.

"You want to consummate the deal now?"

The word consummate brought back memories of marriage and loss and renewed his determination to get this conversation back on a rational track. He slammed out of the Jag.

Circling the car, he yanked her door open. "Come on."

Her head snapped back, and her startled gaze settled on him. "I . . . uh . . ."

"For heaven's sake," he muttered as he leaned over her to unbuckle her seat belt and then help her from the car. "I'm not going to rape you. We need to talk, and now is as good a time as any."

He slid his arm around her waist to lead her to the elevator. He never touched her, and now he couldn't seem to stop. He pulled her closer until their bodies touched torso to thigh, teasing himself and tormenting her. She deserved it.

She did a pretty good imitation of a walking statue, holding herself completely stiff beside him.

And she says she wants me to be her lover, he thought with a derision that bordered on disappointment.

He leaned around her to push the button for the elevator. The force he used to press the small white square said an awful lot about his mood. None of it good. He used the keypad to access the penthouse level, and the elevator began its silent ascent.

She moved like she was going to pull away, but he tugged her closer. "If you're going to be my lover, you'd better get used to me touching you."

She sucked in air, but didn't attempt to move away again, and it took only a few seconds for him to regret his impulse to hold her. She felt way too good next to his body. His sex stood to attention and saluted the soft floral scent of her skin as it teased his senses. He gritted his teeth.

Her breath was coming in short pants, and her heartbeat was visible in a tantalizing pulse on her neck.

He wanted to kiss that pulse, wanted to taste the smooth, creamy skin. He let his gaze slide to the perfect small curves of her breasts encased in the shimmering moss-colored satin of her bodice. And damn if he didn't regret the impulse when the small shoals created by hard nipples caught and held his attention with the power of a mind magnet.

She was excited.

So was he. Aching with it. Hot and hard flesh strained against his pants, and he wanted to take her body and make it his against the wall of the small enclosure.

Thankfully the elevator doors opened at that moment. He dragged her into his apartment and peeled away from her immediately, needing to breathe air not scented by her feminine fragrance.

It didn't help.

He turned on her and glared. "Tell me you didn't mean that about sharing my bed."

She swallowed and shook her head.

"Good. Now, let's discuss this like mature adults."

Her hands fisted at her sides, and she took a deep breath. "I did mean it."

His temper exploded. "Damn it, Phoebe—"

"Don't swear at me, Rand Alexander," she interrupted before he could warm to his tirade. "If you will remember, you were the one who told my great-aunt and your brother you intended to take me to bed."

"I'm not some da—" He cut himself off and was angry with himself for doing so. *"I am not a stud for hire.* If you want to pay a man to warm your bed, I suggest you try an escort service."

She visibly recoiled from his words, but the stubborn little chin came up again. "May I remind you that the terms of this deal were your idea? You said you would give me a week in your bed if I gave you the deed to Luna Island."

"I was pissed. I didn't mean it."

"Were you?" She looked down her nose at him, which was no mean feat considering how much smaller she was. "It was always my understanding that a businessman's word was his bond."

"This is not a business deal!"

She jumped at his bellow, and he sighed. She was nuts, but he didn't want to scare her. He liked Phoebe. It wasn't her fault he wanted her in a way that he couldn't deal with.

"Look, Phoebe, this is crazy. I'll pay you fair market value for the island and a percentage of the minerals extracted." Repeating the offer didn't do him a bit of good.

She shook her head vehemently. "We've already agreed on terms."

"Are you so desperate to lose your virginity, you're willing to blackmail a man into taking you to bed?" It was a stab in the dark, but her wild blush confirmed his guess.

She glared at him. "I repeat: the terms of the deal were your idea."

"Honey, this is not the way you want to lose your cherry."

Phoebe felt like exploding. "What would you know about it? You've had more women than restaurant lunches in the last year. I'm twenty-five years old. I've been engaged, but I've never gone to bed with anyone, and that is going to change."

"Not with me, it won't."

She stared at him, all of her anger fading fast as reality finally intruded on the madness that had held her in its grip since he had made the unbelievable offer in the first place.

What was she doing?

She couldn't blackmail or bribe Rand into making love to her. Not even for the price of an island he wanted.

A man had to desire a woman to sleep with her, and Rand did not want Phoebe. Contrary to his earlier assurances, he didn't even really see her as a woman. Certainly he realized she was a female of his species, but that was clinical. He had no desire for her femininity.

Why should he?

She wasn't the type of woman to inspire uncontrollable passion, or even mild desire, apparently.

Carter hadn't wanted her either.

They'd been engaged, but he had never attempted to cross the line she'd set during their courtship.

Without saying another word, she spun on her heel and headed for the elevator. She pressed the button and said something truly shocking under her breath when she realized it was in use and she would have to wait for it.

"Where are you going?"

He was right behind her, the animal magnetism of his body drawing her in cruel mockery.

"Back to the reception." She couldn't believe she'd left in the first place. As an organizer, she was responsible for making sure everything ran smoothly. And Rand was supposed to make a speech later.

"Like hell."

She ignored his temper and willed the elevator doors to open.

"You are not going to bed with my brother."

She wondered if she was going to make it into the elevator before the tears came. They were burning her eyes and making her throat ache from holding them in. Why in the world had she fallen in love with a man incapable of feeling that emotion? And what cruel trick of providence had decided her body would crave him like an addict craved his next fix?

His big hand landed on her bare skin, burning her with sexual energy he was oblivious to, and she silently cursed the off-the-shoulder style of her gown. It was all she could do not to turn around and beg him to put her body out of its misery, to have sex with her even if he couldn't love her. The pride her aunt had accused her of nursing earlier was in a puddle of need around her feet.

"I'm not letting you leave while you're talking crazy like this, honey."

The bell dinged, and the doors to the elevator started to slide open. Rand reached around her and pressed a button that closed them again.

"Why did you do that?" she asked in a voice strained by the pain she was holding inside.

She should be used to losing, but it still hurt. She'd lost her parents, first to wanderlust and then to death. Then her uncle had died, leaving her Luna Island and a heart that missed the kind old man. Carter had done his flit a year later.

She'd never even had Rand to begin with.

Her current pain was all out of proportion.

"We're not done talking."

She'd already humiliated herself in front of him, exposing her desperation and her desire. She could not stand adding to that humiliation by losing control of her emotions, and she was terrified that was exactly what would happen if she didn't get out of there right now.

"Yes, we are." She stabbed at the down button. The doors opened.

Rand pressed the close button.

"Open it." Her voice was shrill, even to her own ears, but she was desperate to get out of there.

"No."

She spun to face him, dislodging his hand from her shoulder. "You have no right to keep me here."

"I'm not going to let you leave until you've calmed down."

"You mean until you're sure I won't hand my island over

His emotions weren't involved, not like hers. If they
, he wouldn't be fighting the idea of going to bed
so hard. She didn't care.

vanted him for so long, it was an ache inside her she
vould never be assuaged. Wasn't a taste of heaven
a lifetime without knowing the kind of passion
re he could give her?

g her with his understanding and silent compassion,
d in when Carter had taken off. Rand's friendship
er pride. He'd escorted her to social functions, in-
cochair committees with him and kept her mind
things besides her unexpected single status.

y, her mind and her emotions had become fo-
m. He had never realized it, and she had done
hange that. Until tonight.

, and hard flesh moved against her, startling her
ing proportions.

red, her heart pounding so loud it was a drum-
d. "You do want me."

sounded incredible to her, the concept even

ands settle against his chest, one right over his
ke me. *Please.*"

to Carter?" she taunted, relieved that anger had superceded
the urge to cry.

"He wants the island, not you. Don't you see that?"

Rand sounded furious, and she could imagine why. He
was convinced she was going to sign the mineral rights over
to his half brother.

"That makes two of you, then, doesn't it?"

Frustration burned in his silver-gray eyes. "It's not the
same thing, damn it."

They both wanted the island. Neither man wanted her
personally. The only difference was that with Carter, she didn't
care. Rand's rejection was shredding a heart already tender-
ized by watching him flirt with another woman.

For the sake of what was left of her pride, she had to get
away from him. She spun around again and stabbed the elevator button. It took two tries because once again, tears were
blurring her vision, but she got it. The doors slid open just as
she went airborne.

Two strong arms supported her against the rock-solid
wall of his chest. "You're not leaving."

Trying to push herself out of his arms, she glared up at
him through the wetness in her eyes. "Put me down, Rand."

His hold tightened, and he shook his head. "You're not
acting rational."

"So you're going to hold me against my will until I do, or
until I agree to sell you the island?" The sarcasm would have
no doubt been more effective if it hadn't been delivered with
a breaking voice.

Something shifted across Rand's features. "Don't cry, baby.
I know seeing Carter again has got you all upset and you're
going a little crazy here, but you'll feel better soon."

He thought seeing Carter again was the reason for her *going
crazy* as he called it? She considered it as a face-saving excuse, but she'd rather be honest and embarrassed than go to

bed that night knowing she was a liar and a coward. Besides, was it really an improvement to be seen as a woman pining after a man who had dumped her years ago?

"Carter doesn't have anything to do with this."

Rand's expression said he didn't believe her. Maybe she *was* going crazy, but how could the guy be *that* dense?

She needed to get herself under control. Now. Or he wasn't going to let her go. And she *had* to get away from him.

Taking a deep breath, she concentrated on blinking back her tears. She reached inside his tux for the crisp, clean handkerchief she knew he always had on the inside pocket of any suit jacket. He went absolutely still as she fumbled for the hidden pocket in the silk lining. She pulled the handkerchief out and started mopping up her face. Tempted to hide behind it, she nevertheless crushed it into a soggy ball in her hand. She hated crying in front of other people.

"You can put me down now."

"Can I?" His voice sounded odd.

Probably because he was still worried about her going off the sexual deep end with Carter.

"Yes. I'm not going to give in to any further bouts of terminal stupidity tonight." She couldn't quite meet his eyes, but she patted his chest to reassure him. If the pat was more a caress, he had only himself to blame, holding her so close. "I promise."

"I wish you hadn't done that."

Now he sounded really peculiar. She forced herself to make eye contact. His glittered strangely.

"Done what? You mean used your handkerchief? Don't you have another one?" Of course he did. They were in his apartment after all. What was his problem?

"You touched me."

"You picked me up. Touching you is sort of unavoidable."

"So is this."

"Wha—" But his lips cut off the rest of her question.

Hot, male lips that caught her m
the sexiest kiss she'd ever experie
like a scoop of vanilla ice cream in
decadence of his kiss drowned he
not breach her interior. His lips
his sexual expertise, but it didn
nique. It felt personal and wo
tween.

She was just coming to ac
when he pulled back and set
ally should not have done th

The kiss had been far to
couldn't say a word, but he
no *should not have* about

He gently set her on he
tipsy than she'd ever gott
steadied her with his ha

Neither of them spo
forced out the question
did you do that?"

She just might die i

His head tilted fo
and he shook it as if

Bewildered by w
still pulsing desire,
hair. "But you don

His head snapp
ingly savage expr
body against his.
teeth, "too dam

Then he gav
himself against

He meant i

He really

She could

Chapter Four

Rand made a primitive noise deep in his throat he didn't even recognize as his own. Damn if he didn't sound more like an animal preparing to devour its prey than mate, but she made him crazy.

Take me. The words spun through his mind, breaking the last barrier of resistance as his mouth did exactly that. This wasn't just giving in to the need to taste, but a full-out claim staking that he didn't want to analyze. He captured her lips, asserting sexual rights with primal instincts no modern man should admit to.

They were soft. Soft and sweet and sexy. She didn't seem to know what to do with them though, so he licked the seam of her mouth with the tip of his tongue. She moaned faintly, and her lips parted. He took possession of the inside of her mouth, tasting her, making her taste him.

Her fingers curled into the fine fabric of his shirt, her body pressed against his, and her mouth molded to his own.

She didn't suck on his tongue, but she let him suck on hers and made an ageless sound of feminine need when he did it.

His hands moved around to her back, finding the zipper for her dress and sliding it down with ease. He pressed her away from him slightly so he could get the dress off of her, but she shook her head, her eyes unfocused and wild.

"No, I . . ."

"I want you naked."

She stopped fighting to get back in his arms and stared at him, hazel eyes glinting gold and rounded with shock.

"Contrary to what your aunt probably told you, honey, you have to take off your clothes to make love."

Her cheeks went pink, and her hands flew to the bodice of her dress as if it were at risk of falling down. Which it had been.

He stepped closer and bent down to kiss her again, his fingers tugging at the fabric held so tightly in her hands. "Come on," he said against her lips, "let it go. I want to feel your skin against me."

He deepened the kiss, and her grip went slack, giving him a heady sense of power. She responded to him like no other woman ever had. He reveled in the knowledge as he pulled on the dress until it fell in a pool of moss green chiffon and satin at her feet. He teased himself by trying to imagine what she looked like without actually letting himself see her. He skimmed the curve of her waist with his fingertips, and what he felt there paralyzed him. Boning. Satin.

Oh, man. No way.

He pulled back and looked. And looked. And looked some more.

It was.

A corselette and stockings. Her small breasts plumped up from the ivory satin cups, their top edges barely concealing her nipples.

Her panties were stretchy lace in the same color, the see-through pattern giving him a perfect view of honey gold curls.

"I thought you were a virgin." His voice came out a croak, but shock was a mild word for what he was feeling right now.

She chewed on the bottom lip he'd been kissing seconds before. "I am."

"You sure as hell don't dress like a woman who doesn't have a lover."

She blushed again. "I like to read the Victoria's Secret catalogue."

"Honey, you're not reading it, you're wearing it."

"It's dumb. I know. Nobody sees it but me—"

He had to interrupt there. "And me."

If anything, her face turned redder. "And you. Anyway, it's a total waste of money, but I like the way sexy lingerie makes me feel."

He could not hold back from touching her one more second. He reached out and brushed the upper swell of her breast. "Tell me how it makes you feel."

She shivered, her breath quickening. "Like a woman. Feminine."

"Don't you feel like a woman all the time?" She was everything female to him.

She surprised him when she shook her head. "For a while, I felt like a robot who wore skirts. That's when I started wearing the lingerie. It reminded me that I was a woman, not just an automaton."

He didn't want them to, but her words touched something deep inside him. He couldn't let that happen.

He yanked her toward him, not hard, but with purpose she could not mistake. His lips hovered a breath above hers. "I guarantee you are going to feel like a woman tonight."

Then he kissed her, and this time, he made no allowances for her innocence. He took her mouth like the marauding shark he was. She needed to know she could not build sand castles and dreams around him. He was never going down that route again.

He could give her sex and plenty of it, but nothing else.

He showed her with the merciless touch of his lips, the

ruthless way he bared her breasts to his touch. Her nipples were hard, and he made them harder. Playing with them. Pinching them. Rolling them between his thumb and forefinger.

She didn't fight him. Not even for a second.

She just melted into him and kissed him back.

His sex was so hard, he wasn't sure they'd make it into the bedroom for their first time.

He scooped her up with his arm under her bottom and fit her feminine core against him.

She was hot, humid.

Her arms wrapped around his neck, and she hugged his face to hers, kissing him with the same feverish need he felt.

A small ding registered dimly, then the whoosh of elevator doors. He was whipping his tuxedo coat off and around her almost nude body when he heard his half brother's voice from behind them.

"I've got to hand it to you, Rand. You don't lose any time closing a deal, do you?"

Rand spun around, shoving Phoebe behind him.

Carter's blue eyes glinted with what appeared to be humor, and they weren't looking at him. "With legs like those, Phoebe, honey, a man has to wonder why you hide them in long skirts and slacks all the time."

She squeaked in distress from her hiding place at Rand's back, and it was all he could do not to shove his fist into Carter's pretty-boy face. But in order to take a swing at his brother, he'd have to move away from Phoebe, and she now had a death grip on the back of his shirt with one fist.

"How the hell did you get up here?"

"Security keyed me up. I'm family, don't you know?"

"You're a pain in the ass."

"But you don't deny I'm family."

The lack of mockery in his brother's voice bothered Rand. It was almost as if Carter wanted to acknowledge their relationship in some concrete way. Not likely.

"What are you doing here?"

"Did you really expect me to let you get away with kidnapping Phoebe from the reception?"

Rand shrugged. "No. You want the island too much, but I didn't expect security to let you up."

It was Carter's turn to shrug. "Being a Sloane still has some clout in this town. But I didn't come just because of the island. I'm also Phoebe's friend."

"And you were worried about her?" Rand wasn't buying it.

"She's not exactly in your league."

Phoebe leaned around Rand, the hand not attached to the back of his shirt holding the tuxedo coat tightly around her. She looked damn cute.

"Let's get a couple things straight. What I do with my personal life is no one else's business but mine. Furthermore, I left the reception of my own free will. Rand did not *kidnap* me."

"Your aunt is convinced he did."

"My aunt is prejudiced."

Carter's lips tilted in a half smile. "I did notice that, but she's also worried that if Rand isn't there to give his speech and present the award, the gossip will ruin you."

Rand stiffened and muttered a favorite four-letter word that had Phoebe smacking him in the back. He'd forgotten the award, and he had no desire to see her the center of scandalous gossip. He was much more interested in seeing her naked in the center of his big bed.

He flicked the cuff of his shirt back and looked at the time. He was due to present the award in thirty minutes. It was a fifteen-minute drive to the hotel. "I'll be there."

Carter nodded. "I figured you would, but Phoebe had better be there, too, if you don't want her aunt to be your next visitor tonight."

"I'll have a word with security about keying unwelcome visitors of any kind to the penthouse level."

Carter shrugged. "Do you really think that will work in keeping Mz. Emmaline from reaching her niece if she wants to?"

"Hell. Probably not. Phoebe will be with me. Now that you've done your good deed . . . get out."

Instead of looking offended by his dismissal, Carter looked damned amused. "You're not very hospitable, Rand."

"Sorry, I wasn't raised in the blue-blooded environment you were. Social niceties aren't my thing."

Carter's jaw tightened at the reference to their separate upbringings, but then he sighed. "No. You weren't. I'm not sure which one of us paid the higher price for it, though."

"It's a little late to be worrying about that now."

"Maybe. If I were the one who screwed up, but neither of us is responsible for the stupidity of our father."

What was going on? "Do you think I'll share mineral rights with you if you attempt a replay of Happy Families?" He'd learned a long time ago not to trust anyone with the last name Sloane, and that included his father.

A small fist landed against his right shoulder blade. "That was uncalled for, Rand. Carter's your brother, and I, for one, am glad somebody is finally waking up to that fact in a meaningful way."

"Stay out of this, Phoebe. It's none of your business." He knew he sounded harsh and figured his words probably hurt her feelings.

The way she let go of his shirt and stepped away from him said as much.

"Why don't you put your dress back on and I'll take you back to the reception?" Carter fairly oozed concerned charm, and Rand took a step toward him, his hand curling into a fist.

"Phoebe's not going anywhere with you."

Phoebe glared at Rand's back, hurt by his brutal dismissal of her opinion a moment ago and angry that he thought he had the right to dictate to her after it. Sure, he'd been talking to Carter, but the effect had been the same. Bossing her around.

"I can speak for myself."

Rand turned around to face her, his expression hard and accusing. "Are you saying you want to leave with him?"

She pulled his coat more tightly around her as if that could protect her from the heat of his anger. "I'm saying that it is my decision to make."

"Then make it. Either you go with him, or you stay with me."

Did he have to make it sound as though the choice had so little import to him? But then what did she expect? He'd been fighting any move in a more personal direction in their relationship for the past hour. Maybe he saw this as an easy way out of what they'd almost done.

She glared at him, as much for what she was thinking as for what he'd said.

He spun on his heel and headed toward the bedroom. "I'm going to change into another shirt and dinner jacket. If you're here when I come out, I'll assume you decided to stay with me."

And it didn't matter one way or another to him either.

"Don't you believe it."

She'd muttered it under her breath, but Carter had heard. "He's mad, and when he gets mad, he says stupid stuff. He's in there right now wanting to kick himself for leaving the field open to me so easily."

She'd love to believe that was true; even more she'd like to believe it was because of her and not Luna Island. She wasn't that much of a dreamer. "What makes you so sure?"

"We're a lot alike. That's how I know he's too proud to come back out and ask you to stay, even if that's what he wants to do."

"Do you want me to stay with him?" She couldn't make out what was motivating Carter right now.

He grimaced. "I don't know. The Phoebe I left behind four years ago would be no match for my older brother, but you've changed, and I'm just beginning to realize how much. Maybe you don't need my protection from him."

"I don't, but what about the lithium?"

"I want it. I won't lie about that, but it's pretty obvious there's something between you and Rand, and I figure I owe you both enough, I shouldn't try too hard to screw it up."

Was she hearing what she thought she was hearing? Carter cared about Rand. "You did come back to renew family ties."

Carter was right. He and Rand were a lot alike. The way he went stonelike and stoic was very reminiscent of his brother to her.

"I came back for a lot of reasons. Not least of which was to tell you I'm sorry."

She was no longer interested in apologies from her ex-fiancé. That part of her life had been over for a long time. She was much more concerned with whether or not Rand was going to follow through on his promise to make her feel like a woman.

Nevertheless, she said, "You were right. We weren't ready to make that kind of commitment. It took me a while to get there, but in the end I was grateful you backed out of our wedding."

"I'm glad."

"Still here?"

Phoebe couldn't tell if Rand was speaking to her or his brother.

"You changed pretty fast," Carter mocked.

Rand didn't reply, but his molten gaze settled on Phoebe. "Maybe you'd like to put *your* clothes on, unless you enjoy entertaining my brother while you're practically naked."

If she didn't know better, she'd think he was jealous.

Carter laughed. "You'd better put your dress on before the green-eyed monster eats my brother alive."

Rand swept her dress up off the floor and handed it to her. "Get dressed. As it is, we're cutting it to the wire on time."

"You could go ahead and I could follow with Carter." Even as she made the suggestion, she realized it wasn't a good one. If she let Rand go now, would he change his mind about making love to her? Had he already?

"I'll wait."

She was too relieved he apparently wanted her to stick with him to take issue with his surly tone. "I'll just be a minute."

She rushed to the bathroom where she scrambled back into her dress. Thank goodness for the wrinkle resistance of the fabric, she thought. A few touches to her hair and she looked almost as she had when Rand had taken her from the hotel.

She came back out to the living room to find Carter gone. "Your brother left?"

"Yes." Rand turned and pressed the button for the elevator and then fixed his silent scrutiny on her.

By the time the elevator doors slid open, she was feeling very self-conscious. "Is there something the matter with my dress?"

"Just that it's covering your body."

Heat spread up her limbs and settled in her cheeks. "Oh."

"It's a beautiful dress, but I'd rather be seeing what is underneath."

"Then you haven't changed your mind?"

"I want you. That isn't going to change until I've had you."

Did that mean he thought that once they made love, he would get over his attraction for her? The thought was a depressing one, so she ignored it. "When?"

He didn't pretend to misunderstand what she was asking. "We'll be coming back here after I make my speech and you explain things to your aunt. By the way, I've got a trip I need to make to North Carolina to check on one of my suppliers.

You can come with me. We'll fly out tomorrow and be gone for three days."

"You want me to go away with you?" She'd never even considered such a move.

"You said you wanted a week in my bed. Three days of this week I'll be in North Carolina. If you want to be in my bed, you'll be there too."

The mind boggled at the prospect of explaining to her aunt about spending the night with Rand, much less a three-day jaunt with him to another state.

"Is it going to be a problem?" he asked.

"I hadn't considered traveling with you."

"Well?" He wasn't giving any quarter.

While her volunteer job at the library often took more than forty hours a week, her schedule was flexible. "No. It won't be a problem."

Aunt Emmaline's reaction to Phoebe's return to the charity reception was unqualified relief. It turned to absolute dismay when Phoebe told her she was flying to North Carolina with Rand in the morning.

"You cannot seriously be considering spending three days with that man."

No, she was going to spend the week with him, but she didn't say that to her great-aunt. Instead she reached out and squeezed the older woman's hand. "I love you, Aunt Emmaline, but I've got to live my own life, and the key here is live. When I'm with Rand I don't feel like an extra person in the world."

The older woman's pale blue gaze softened. "Darling, I always wanted you."

But her parents hadn't and Carter hadn't. Rand did, even if it was temporary. "I know, but please try to understand."

"I don't want you hurt."

"I would hurt more if I didn't go." She didn't deny that pain might eventually come; she couldn't.

It was all too likely.

Rand chose that moment to join them. He handed Phoebe the keys to his car. "Take my car and go pack what you need for the trip. I'll hold the fort here while you're gone. Just buzz my cell when you're out front."

She took the keys, avoiding her aunt's eyes.

"My niece is not one of your flighty fancy pieces."

She had to give him credit. Rand didn't even crack a smile at her aunt's old-fashioned terminology. He simply inclined his head, his expression grave. "No, ma'am. She's special."

Phoebe's heart contracted at the words, but she didn't read too much into them. Rand was trying to smooth the way with her aunt for her, and she appreciated it. He could have just blabbed out their deal and shocked Aunt Emmaline into heart failure.

He walked her to the hotel foyer.

"Aunt Emmaline took that better than I expected."

"We've been friends for years. I don't think the deepening of that friendship comes as a total shock."

It certainly wouldn't for her aunt, who knew Phoebe's feelings for Rand.

She nodded and turned to leave, but he stayed her with a hand on her wrist. "It's just sex. You know that? I'm not taking you to bed just to get the deed to the island. I want you, but it's physical. I don't have anything left to give when it comes to love and happily ever after. Got it?"

Just knowing it wasn't all part of a business deal was a huge relief. She hadn't expected him to admit undying love. "I've got it."

He leaned over and kissed her. "Good. I'll see you in a while."

"Yes."

His lips claimed hers again, hard and brief. "Until then."

Her hand came up to cover her mouth, as if she could hold the kiss to her lips with the press of her fingers. What did a woman pack for a week with Rand Alexander?

Chapter Five

Rand waited outside the hotel with all the impatience of a horny teen. He wanted sex with Phoebe until he was aching with it. He'd spent the last couple of years sublimating his desire for her. Now that he'd allowed it to surface completely, it had become a force of hurricane proportions. He couldn't believe he'd agreed to a one-week affair. Could seven days and nights be enough to sate the hunger she generated in him?

He doubted it, but the risk of letting the relationship go longer than that was too great to even contemplate.

Not making love with her was no longer an option he could live with. He wanted her too much, and he'd be dead and in the ground before he let his half brother have another chance at hurting Phoebe.

Which said what for the emotional detachment so necessary to his own peace of mind?

Rand was glaring and looked about as approachable as a grizzly bear woken from his nap when Phoebe pulled his Jaguar next to the curb in front of the hotel. She clicked the unlock button and was mildly surprised when he slid into the passenger seat without protest.

"Have you got everything?"

"Yes." She'd even stopped at the twenty-four-hour drugstore and bought a box of condoms. It was a big box, and remembering how he had felt against her earlier, she'd also bought the larger size.

"Then let's go."

He sounded more like they were headed to another committee meeting than back to his apartment to make love for the first time. Maybe it was that unmomentous to him.

It wasn't to her, and she grimaced as she ground the gears, pulling away from the curb. Maybe she should have asked him to drive. Her palms were sticky, and her heart was beating so fast, she was feeling a little dizzy.

But he didn't say anything about the ground gears, and she made it to his apartment building without further incident.

When she parked, he got out, came around and opened her door before opening the trunk and pulling out her luggage. He carried it all to the elevator, and she followed, finding it impossible to break the deafening silence that had fallen between them.

By the time they reached his apartment, she was more nervous than she'd ever been in her life.

He went straight back to his bedroom, and she followed, feeling more like she was walking to her doom than approaching her first experience with true and fulfilling passion.

The midnight blue and cream of the room was softened slightly by the recessed lighting, but she still felt the powerful impact of the masculinity of the furnishings. The dark wood and stark colors made her feel as though she'd entered an alien world.

Rand dropped her cases on a padded bench at the foot of his oversized king bed and turned to face her. "You changed your clothes." He made it sound like an accusation.

"It's more comfortable." She'd taken off her formal gown and put on a long denim skirt and lightweight tan sweater set.

"Did you change what's underneath?"

The way he was looking at her made her feel as if he could already see for himself. It certainly felt like his eyes were burning through her clothes. "No."

"Let me see."

"You want me to take my clothes off?" she squeaked.

"Yes."

"Right now?"

"It would make what we're going to do a lot easier," he said dryly. Unemotionally.

And she just couldn't do it. "No."

His brows rose at that. "You want me to have sex with you with your clothes on? I didn't expect a virgin to have any fetishes."

This was not going to work. She wanted him, but his mockery and lack of any discernable emotion made it clear that making love to her meant nothing to him. She could accept that it was just sex, but not that it was *negligible* sex. "You're doing it on purpose, aren't you?" she demanded, the tether on her emotions frayed and breaking. "You don't want to make love anymore, and you're making fun of me so I'll leave. Well, it worked. I don't want you touching me."

And she didn't, not when it meant humiliating herself in the process. She'd had enough of that tonight to last a lifetime.

She was halfway out the bedroom door when two strong hands grabbed her from behind and spun her to face him. "I'm not making fun of you, Phoebe." He touched her face, his expression without humor and almost scary. "I want you too much to be charm personified right now. I'm dying for another glimpse of you in your sexy lingerie, and maybe it's made me a little crazy."

"It has?"

"Yeah."

Crazy she understood because she'd been acting insane since he caught her spouting off to her aunt earlier that evening.

"I brought a nightgown," she blurted out.

The corner of his lips tilted. "You won't need it."

"But I . . ." She'd thought if she could change in the bathroom or something, she could make the transition to bed without giving in to her nerves and running for the hills.

His finger pressed against her lips. "Shh . . . It's going to be all right."

Then he kissed her, and it wasn't like the kisses before. As much as he said he wanted her, his lips were gentle and coaxing, drawing forth her inexperienced passion when she thought those feelings had been frozen by his seeming indifference.

He tasted her, almost tenderly running his tongue over her lips, sensitizing them.

Her eyes slid shut, and she parted her mouth, sneaking a taste of him with the tip of her own tongue. His big body shuddered, and he swept her into his arms.

She expected to be laid on his bed, was in fact looking forward to it, but he stood her on her feet again.

She looked down and saw that he'd placed her on a footstool. Her gaze flew up to his, but he wasn't looking at her face. His attention was fixed on her breasts where hard nipples were outlined by the thin fabric of her sweater set.

He brushed them with the backs of his hands, and they tightened to a point between pain and pleasure.

"You're sensitive there."

"Y-yes . . ."

"I like that." His voice caressed nerve endings not exposed to his touch. "And I like touching you."

She cried out as he caught her nipples between two fingers and squeezed.

"I want to taste you, too. You are going to love having my mouth on you." His smile was all predatory male. "But first we've got to get your clothes off."

At least this time it was *we*, not *take your clothes off*.

He reached around her, and she felt the button and zipper on her skirt give. He tugged at it, and the denim slid down her thighs, exposing her stockings and the bottom half of her corselette. She gasped as it fell to the floor, making a pool of fabric around the feet of the small footstool.

Then his hands went to the hem of her top, and she grabbed his wrists.

He looked at her then, his eyes hotter than molten metal. "Let me."

"*You're* still dressed."

"You aren't ready to see me naked yet."

It sounded like a threat, and she swallowed. "Are you very big?"

"We'll fit, that's all that matters."

"How can you be so sure?"

"You're going to have to trust me on this."

She nodded, but trepidation was sliding down her spine like a wet icicle on a glacier. She shivered.

"Kiss me, Phoebe."

"You want *me* to kiss *you?*"

He leaned down until his lips were almost touching hers. "Yes." Warm air from his mouth brushed over hers.

Suddenly kissing him seemed like the only thing she wanted from life, and she pressed her mouth to his. She felt the contact all the way to the core of her. She let go of his wrists to tunnel her fingers into his hair. She latched on to the glossy black strands and moved her mouth over his with more enthusiasm than expertise.

He didn't seem to mind her lack of technique. His lips parted, and his tongue teased her. She let him into her mouth, and he drew her into a mating dance with their tongues that had her losing all sense of reality.

He pulled his mouth away, and she whimpered. He unhooked her hands from his hair in order to pull off her sweater. Then he stepped back and just looked at her. She was standing only about six inches above the floor, but she felt more as though she was on a six-foot-tall pedestal. As if she'd been put on display for his express pleasure, which in fact, she had. Rather than being bothered by that, she found it extremely arousing to think that just looking at her gave him pleasure.

His expression mesmerized her into immobility, and she allowed him to look his fill.

She didn't even try to cover her breasts when he reached out and slid the cups of her corselette down to expose them completely. He'd had her like this before, and there was something about the way he looked at her that made her feel both proud and excited.

His fingertip teased her right nipple, the sensation a thousand times more impacting without the layers of her clothes between them.

She groaned.

"Do you like that, baby?"

"*Yes.*"

His left hand joined his right, and both her nipples were subjected to the same sensual torture. She felt wetness and heat between her legs. She pressed her thighs together, but the relief was very short lived. Within seconds, it just seemed to make it worse.

"*Rand.*"

"What's the matter?" His voice wasn't his usual smooth

drawl, but had a guttural quality that said he was affected, too.

"I need . . ." She didn't know how to say what she needed.

"What do you need? Tell me."

She had never indulged in sex talk before and wasn't sure she was ready for her first try at it. "I can't."

"You can." His fingers stopped moving, and she wanted to scream with frustration.

"You said you wanted to taste them!"

"Do *you* want me to?"

"*Yes.*"

His mouth lowered until his lips were barely touching the turgid peaks.

"Please, Rand."

His tongue flicked out and licked her like an ice-cream cone.

A long, low moan snaked out of her throat.

He did it again, treating her oversensitized flesh like the cherry on top of a sundae. He even nipped it, making her scream and arch toward the heat of his mouth. He sucked her into scorching wetness, making an animalistic sound of satisfaction.

It was too much, but she would die if he stopped. She wanted more, needed more and said so in a voice that echoed off the ceiling.

He released her nipple with an audible pop and nipped it once more before raising his head to kiss her again, this time with a carnality that could not be mistaken for anything but a prelude to her complete and total surrender.

His left hand was still playing with her now aching nipple, but his right hand slid down her back until his fingertip was pressing between her tightly clenched buttocks. He pressed inward, caressing her in a shockingly intimate way. His finger moved inexorably toward the heart of her. Making no allowance for the tight clasp of her flesh, it forged a secret path.

Down it went, until the outer lips of her feminine center were parted and his fingertip had slipped just inside her, giving her her very first taste of a man's possession. He pushed her forward, into him, until the front of her mound nestled intimately against his rock-hard sex while he continued his exploration from the back with that insidious finger.

Rand wanted to strip off his clothes, tear Phoebe's sexy lace panties from her body and bury himself inside her so deep, she'd think he was a part of her. She was soaking wet, and the hot flesh surrounding his finger was as slick and swollen as any man could want before getting inside his woman.

And, damn, did he want to do that.

He penetrated her with his finger a little deeper, sinking into the clasping flesh of her sex up to his first knuckle. She tried to arch forward, away from his finger, while a small sound of distress went from her mouth to his.

He rubbed his cock against her mound, reveling in the way her entire body went stiff at the contact. But far from straining away, she pushed herself more firmly against him. Her mouth tore away from his, and she panted, her entire upper body flushed with desire. She was so sexy, more sensual than any woman he'd ever bedded, and he hadn't done half of what he planned to do to her.

His finger pressed more firmly into her until he hit a barrier he knew had to be crossed that night before she could truly become his.

Temporarily.

He couldn't forget that. This was a one-week gig. No white roses. No forever promises. Just sex. Sex that was likely to take the top of his head off, but it wasn't love. It couldn't be. He didn't have that left to give anymore.

Her head came up. "It hurts, Rand."

"I'm sorry." He stopped moving his finger, but he knew to take her where he was going to take her tonight, he would have to hurt her a little.

She squirmed against him. "It's not that bad."

"I don't want it to hurt at all, baby, but I don't know any other way."

Her eyes misted over with tears, and she smiled. "I like it when you call me baby."

"I'm glad." He rubbed himself against her, and she began to shiver uncontrollably. She was close. He knew she was close, and he was going to tip her right over.

He moved his finger in and out, tortured by the feel of her wet, velvety skin clasping him so tight.

He slowly withdrew his finger, and she moaned.

"It's okay. Trust me. I want to make you feel good."

"That did feel good."

"This will feel better." He pressed his thumb inside her swollen, humid flesh and slid his index finger forward until he brushed her small, inflamed clitoris.

Her shivering intensified. A few more strokes and she cried out, her body arching in one long spasm of pleasure. Her inner flesh contracted around his thumb, and it was all he could do not to complete the possession of her body with his throbbing sex buried deep inside her. All at once, she collapsed against him. He held her, caressing her through the aftershocks, but careful not to send her over the edge again.

He wanted to be inside her the next time, and his cock was straining for release. When he knew she'd come down enough to stand on her own, he pulled away from her, not letting her step off the stool.

She stared at him, her eyes unfocused, her beautiful lips swollen from his kisses.

"Stay there." He wanted to look at her while he took his clothes off.

Her brows came together. "Why?"

He almost laughed at the naive question, but he hurt too much to laugh. "I want to see you."

She was still wearing her shoes, a pretty tame pair of pumps, but very sexy with the stockings, corselette and lace panties. Her gorgeous little breasts were still fully exposed above the satin he'd pushed down, the cups making a shelf that lifted the creamy white skin in a very tantalizing way.

She opened her mouth to say something, maybe to argue, but he took off his jacket and then his shirt in short order. She stood there, her lips slightly parted, her attention completely focused on his body as he removed his clothes.

When he peeled away the silk boxers, she gasped and shook her head. "It's not going to work. That's a lot bigger than your finger."

This time he did laugh, a short, pain-filled chuckle. "You're just going to have to trust my experience on this one."

Her head averted, her gaze shifting away from him. "You've been with a lot of women. I must seem pretty gauche in comparison."

Was she crazy? "You're so damn sexy, I'm one stroke away from premature ejaculation."

Her arms wrapped around her middle. "You don't have to say that."

He rolled his eyes. *Women!* They had the strangest ideas, and he just did not have the tact to deal nicely with her bout of insecurity right now. He wanted her too much. "Get on the bed."

That brought her eyes back into contact with his.

He didn't wait for her shock to subside so she could do as he'd said, but stepped forward and swung her up in his arms. "I want you, and I can't wait anymore."

She buried her face in his neck and pressed a small kiss there. "Okay," she whispered.

He could hear the fear in her voice, but the anticipation, too.

He would show her she had nothing to fear from him and everything to look forward to.

Chapter Six

Phoebe clung to Rand as he went to lay her on the bed, the feel of his naked skin against hers the most amazing sensation she'd ever had in her life.

Maybe her lack of practical application in this area was to blame, but every sensory receptor in her body seemed to be on overload from the experience. Full body contact was so intimate, just the *thought* of him fitting inside her was enough to make her shudder.

It would be supremely intimate.

She couldn't help worrying it would be slightly uncomfortable as well. She'd felt really full with just his finger. Maybe she was too tight, and her body wasn't as resilient and stretchable as it would have been if she weren't a virgin. He'd told her to trust him, and she was trying, but it was hard.

"Phoebe."

She opened her eyes to find him looking down at her, an intense expression tightening his features.

She licked her suddenly dry lips. "What?"

"I'm going to make you mine now."

What was she supposed to say to that? Probably something equally erotic and sophisticated, but all she could do was agree. "Okay."

He pulled away from her and leaned over to open his night-stand drawer. She watched in utter fascination as he rolled a condom over his engorged sex. He turned back to her and smiled at her rapt expression. "You can do it next time."

"I don't know how."

"It's not hard. I'm sure you can figure it out, and I'm bound to enjoy you trying."

He wanted her to touch him? She realized she'd whispered the words aloud when his expression turned rapacious.

"Hell, yes. I want your sweet little hands everywhere, and by the time tonight is over they will have been."

"I want that, too," she admitted.

His smile was all-conquering male. "I know."

She laughed at his ego, but her humor fled fast enough when he came back to her on the bed. Without her really un-derstanding how it happened, he divested her of her remain-ing clothes, all the while touching her in ways that were guaranteed to make her crazy.

When she was a trembling, naked mass of nerves lying there on his bed, he came down on top of her again. And this time, her brain did a short-circuit. She lost sense of anything except the feel of his body against hers. She could feel his thighs brushing the inside of her own, the blunt tip of his shaft against her virgin opening, his lips molding hers, his hands exploring excited flesh. Her entire world shrank to physical sensation and a burgeoning of love in her heart that was so overwhelming, she thought she might explode from it.

But no matter how much she longed to cry out her love along with her pleasure, she kept the words locked tight in her throat.

He wanted sex, not emotion.

His pelvis tilted toward her, and it started . . . his posses-sion of her body.

"Does it hurt?" he asked, his voice tight with strain.

How could she answer? It felt like nothing she'd ever known before. Yes, there was some pain, but it was part of a maelstrom of sensations, and she could not distinguish it as separate from the others.

"It doesn't matter," she choked out between panting breaths.

She tipped up toward him, wanting more of him. Needing his complete possession. It seemed to drive him right over the edge, and he plunged deeper into her, breaking through her barrier with one thrust. She screamed. She couldn't help it.

She had no problem distinguishing the feelings now.

"It hurts." She tried to shove him off while doing her best to sink back into the bed away from his marauding flesh. "This is not going to work."

He was about as movable as a rock and definitely as hard as one, but he stopped thrusting.

His shoulders were slick with sweat, the muscles under her hands bulging with the effort to hold still, and his entire body shook with tension. "It's going to work," he ground out.

It was no gentle wooing, but the pain in his expression more than matched her own, and for some reason that made it better. He needed her. He didn't just want to have sex with her. He *needed* it, and that made the pain worth it. She stopped trying to get away from him.

He moved, just a little, and she gasped as she felt a new shaft of pain arc through her.

"You've got to relax." His jaw was so tight, it could have been hewn from marble.

"I don't know how." She was failing him, and she couldn't stand it. She wanted this to work. Wanted it so much, but she couldn't seem to accommodate him like his other lovers must have done.

He didn't say anything, but his mouth lowered, and the lips that pressed against hers were not hard and angry. They weren't even impatient. They were gentle and coaxing, and bit by bit, the rigidity in her body lessened.

"That's it. You can do it, honey." The words of encouragement whispered against her lips were as tantalizing as his kiss. "That's right, relax for me."

Both tender and carnal, his mouth drew forth her passion despite the lingering discomfort. He started another rocking, this time small movements of his hips that left him deeper inside her with each thrust. And far from pain, she felt an indescribable pleasure.

Finally, his pelvis ground into her own, and she felt full, stretched to capacity. She could not move so much as a centimeter with his heavy body pressing hers down and his hardness inside her.

He maneuvered his legs until they were outside hers, pressing her thighs together and her flesh more firmly around his shaft. She whimpered as the movement put him into almost unbearable contact with her clitoris.

"Are you ready?"

For what? But she said, "Yes," because she needed something and was sure he knew what it was.

She was right. He pulled out of her until only the tip of his big erection was still inside her and then plunged back into her. Hard. He did it over and over again, caressing her clitoris the entire time with that granite-hard shaft. She cried out again, but this time from the incredible bliss of it.

She climbed toward that pinnacle he'd given her once already with a speed that left her begging and trying to move under him. She tilted her pelvis, succeeding in moving enough to increase the friction between his flesh and her sweet spot.

He ground his pelvis against her in a circle with each downward thrust, and her fingers gripped his shoulders, her nails digging into the slick skin.

He tore his mouth from hers. "Now, baby. Come with me now!"

And she did.

Pleasure exploded inside her like an atomic bomb while his feral shout of release rang in her ears and his body bowed above hers for endless seconds. He collapsed on top of her, and she hugged him with arms that felt like limp spaghetti.

His face nuzzled next to hers. "Now you're mine."

Tears of happiness blurred her eyes, and she was glad he couldn't see them. "Yes."

"For a week."

Tears of another kind tightened her throat, but she refused to give in to them. A week as his woman was better than a lifetime of loneliness.

"For a week," she repeated.

It shouldn't, but having her agree with the one-week stipulation bothered Rand.

He asked himself what he had expected. She was a twenty-five-year-old woman looking for sexual experience, not a lifetime commitment.

Even if he had that to give her, which he didn't.

Being raised the bastard son of a leading citizen in the small town of New Hope had taught Rand to guard his heart and be wary of any emotion remotely connected to love. Losing Susan and their son had torn what was left of his heart to shreds.

For a long time, he had resisted even Phoebe's nondemanding friendship. Then Carter had taken his flit, and she had been devastated, in need of some kind of support. Rand had felt responsible. It hadn't made any sense. She'd been nothing to him, but he'd suspected he knew why his brother had called off the wedding. Rand had showed him letters that proved beyond the shadow of a doubt that their father had loved his mother, or at least lusted after her, while remaining married for appearances sake to Carter's.

Something had snapped in his brother, and he'd taken off, leaving Phoebe to face a humiliation she had not deserved.

Rand had offered her his friendship, had tried to protect her from the most vicious of the gossip, and she had repaid him with a deep loyalty and caring he refused to examine too closely. He didn't know when he realized she wanted him, or when he'd started wanting her back, but both feelings had grown.

Making love had been inevitable, no matter how much he had tried to avoid it.

He had nothing but sex to give Phoebe, and she deserved so much more. She was beautiful inside and out, but he wasn't risking his heart again.

The least he could do was to make damn sure it was the best sex she would ever know in her life.

Phoebe soaked in the herbal bath Rand had prepared for her. She had no idea where he'd gotten the bath beads that made the water both soft and incredibly soothing to her sore flesh, but she was grateful to whatever angel had provided them. She didn't know if it was Rand's size, or her recent status as a virgin, or the fact they'd made love several times before he allowed her to drift into an exhausted sleep, but she'd woken *very* sore.

Probably, it had been a combination of the three.

All she knew for sure was that when he woke her with his sensual lips on hers, she'd been absolutely certain her week with Rand was bound to be a celibate one. No way could she make love again feeling the way she had.

He'd kept his kisses fairly chaste and fed her breakfast in bed. Afterward, much to her surprise, he had carried her into the bathroom where his whirlpool tub was filled with steaming water tinted a deep emerald green.

Bubbles of fragrant water swirled around her now as the pain between her legs faded to nothing and her aching and strained muscles relaxed.

He'd refused to join her, saying that to do so would defeat the purpose of the bath.

She smiled secretly at the thought of herself as irresistible to Rand. He might be getting the deed to Luna Island in exchange for the week together in bed, but he had not been lying when he said that he *wanted her*. Just her.

It was a heady thought and one she'd much rather dwell on than the one-week time limit to their pseudorelationship.

"Feeling better?"

She opened her eyes at the sound of his voice and smiled up at him. "Yes. Much."

"Good." His white teeth flashed, and gray eyes warmed her with their scrutiny.

She relaxed against the bath pillow behind her. Swirling her hand through the water, she asked, "How did you know about this stuff?"

Rand wasn't the type of man to make love with virgins on a regular basis. His usual date was way too sophisticated for that scenario. On the other hand, maybe other women found his size and stamina a challenge as well.

She hated thinking of him with other lovers and felt her face pull into a frown.

He sat on the edge of the bathtub and leaned over to brush his fingertip along her collarbone. "I called my doctor. He recommended a naturopath who prescribed the bath."

"You must have been up early." And gotten his doctor out of bed, too.

"You were sore when you went to sleep. I knew it would only be worse this morning."

And that bothered him. She could tell. "I was a virgin. It was inevitable that it hurt a little."

He grimaced and withdrew his hand. "I kept at you like a randy teenager."

She reached out and grabbed his hand with her wet one. "I wanted you, too. Every time."

Strong fingers gripped hers. "I know. I still didn't like the idea of you hurting."

"So you fixed it."

He shrugged.

It both touched and embarrassed her that he'd gone to the trouble of calling his doctor. "Thank you, Rand."

He laughed, his expression turning cynical. "It was pure self-interest. I didn't want to spend tonight aching next to a body I wanted to ravish."

What an incredible thought. She could make him ache. "I still think you're a pretty nice guy."

"Don't you believe it. I'm just good at getting what I want."

Right now he wanted her, and she wasn't complaining.

They flew to North Carolina later that morning. Rand spent the day in meetings while Phoebe went shopping in Raleigh's largest mall. She was in the lingerie section of her favorite department store when the idea of a minimakeover took root and grew with the speed of morning glory in the spring.

The salesclerk was pointing out a dress across the aisle from the lingerie department. It was something Phoebe would never have looked at twice. It was too short. Too slinky. Too revealing for her usual mode of dressing.

Usually the idea of drawing any sort of attention to her less than stellar female attributes would have sent her running a mile in the other direction, but Rand liked her small breasts. He had spent hours touching, kissing and praising them the night before.

The thought of exciting him with a sexier way of dressing was way too tantalizing to pass up.

She wasn't going to begin dressing like a tart, but a few skirts that showed her knees and blouses that accentuated her feminine curves would be a good start.

Three hours later, she left the mall with several bags. Some were filled with new, more revealing clothing, and the others attested to her passion for lacy underthings.

She was wearing one of her new purchases when Rand got back to their hotel suite that evening. She felt sexier than she ever had in her life. The short dress of burnished bronze chiffon over satin dipped low in front, exposing the top curve of her breasts. Its full skirt flirted around her thighs in a way none of her old dresses did.

Carter had said she had nice legs.

She hoped Rand agreed. He had certainly enjoyed looking at her in her corselette, and later, after they made love the first time, he'd spent a lot of time just looking at her naked figure on the bed.

She wanted to be beautiful for him. She wanted to dress like a woman who would spend the week in his bed, not her normal conservative self.

His silver eyes flared with desire when he saw her, and she decided the afternoon had been worth it.

She took a deep breath, which stalled somewhere around her windpipe when his gaze zeroed in on her chest pressing against the bodice of her dress. She knew what he could see, because she'd seen them earlier in the mirror. Hard-tipped breasts that exposed the level of her excitement to his knowing gaze.

"Hi."

Tossing his briefcase onto the suite's small sofa, he yanked on his tie. "Hi, yourself. Do we have plans to go out tonight?"

She shook her head. "I ordered room service for later."

His eyes shifted to the standing champagne bucket next to her. Then he looked at her again. "I like the dress."

"I'd hoped you would."

"It's new."

She didn't deny it. "I went shopping this afternoon."

"Did you buy any more sexy underwear?"

It was getting hard to breathe under that stare. "Yes."

"Are you wearing them?"

She shook her head again.

He tossed his tie on top of his briefcase and followed it with his suit coat, then started walking toward her while he unbuttoned his dress shirt. "Does that mean you're wearing boring, cotton panties?"

"Um . . . no."

He reached her, stopping when the toes of his Italian loafers met her sandal-shod feet. "I couldn't stop thinking about you."

He didn't sound happy about the admission.

Maybe it would help him to know it had been mutual. "I kept thinking about you, too."

"Did you?" He played with the hem of her skirt, his fingers sliding underneath and touching the skin of her thigh.

Sensation shot through her intimate flesh, drawing moisture from inside her to warm the cleft between her legs. "Yes." He moved his hand, and her breath hitched. "I wanted to be with you."

Her heart had gone wild, and her breathing was shallow.

His nostrils flared with arousal. "So, if you're not wearing something new, I guess that means you're wearing sexy stuff you already had."

His finger slipped around to flirt with the seam of her legs, only centimeters from flesh aching for his touch.

"No, that's not what it means," she told him on a breathless whisper.

His hand went up, and he barely brushed the soft curls between her legs with the backs of his fingers, but she moaned anyway. It felt so good.

His other hand cupped the back of her head, and he brought

his face down to hers. "There's only one thing I can think of that's more erotic than the thought of you in sexy lingerie."

"There is?" She barely knew what she was saying as her lips brushed his with each movement.

"Yes." He kissed her, softly and slowly. He drew it out until her lips were clinging to his and her fingers were wrapped like manacles around his neck and the wrist next to her head.

He pulled his lips just far enough away to speak again. "The thought of you wearing nothing at all under that dress."

He touched her once more as his lips laid claim to her mouth, this time his entire hand cupping her mound. She arched toward him with a convulsive movement, and he pressed his middle finger between her already swollen and wet lips as she shifted her legs apart in blatant invitation.

He took it with an animal-like growl, touching her humid flesh with intimate strokes that had her gyrating against his hand. Seconds later, he lifted her and set her down on the hard length of his penis. Her body stretched to fit him with much less difficulty than the night before, but it still took some rocking to get him completely inside.

He cupped her bottom and pressed her more firmly against him. "Ride me, Phoebe. Wrap your legs around me and make me come!"

Mindless with unbelievable desire, she obeyed.

She couldn't have done it without him holding her, but he helped her set a pace that rocketed them both to shattering completion in an indecently short span of time.

Sweaty, dazed and still intimately connected to him, she let her head fall against his chest. "I guess you like the shorter dress."

Masculine laughter rumbled in his chest. "You could say that." He rubbed her back with the hand that wasn't support- ing and caressing her bottom. "It's a good thing I had a con-

dom in my pocket, isn't it? I'm not sure I would have made it
to the bedroom for one."

"I suppose a man like you is always prepared."

She felt his lips settle against the top of her head. Then,
"What do you mean, a man like me?"

She rubbed her cheek against his chest, trying not to let
her thoughts bother her. "You date a lot of women."

This time the laugh was short and harsh. "And you think
I sleep with all of them?"

"Don't you?"

"No."

Her head snapped back, and she looked into his fathom-
less eyes. "But I thought . . . Everyone says . . ."

"Gossip is rarely accurate."

"You date gorgeous, sophisticated women."

"And I've slept with a few of them when I needed physical
release, but I'm no more interested in committing sexual sui-
cide than the next guy."

For some totally baffling reason, that reassured her. It shouldn't
matter. He wasn't permanently hers, but she was glad he wasn't
a sexual glutton who had grown jaded on one meaningless
experience after another.

She levered herself more firmly against him and groaned
at the way it felt. "I suppose this means you were due for
some tension release and I caught you at just the right time,
then."

He kicked his shoes and trousers off and started walking
toward the bathroom with her wrapped firmly around him.
"It's not just sexual release."

He said it in such forbidding tones, she didn't dare ask
what it was if it wasn't mere physical relief. Something deep
in her heart rejoiced all the same at the implication she wasn't
a faceless body for him to slake his indiscriminate lust on.

He didn't take a condom in the shower with them, but he

Chapter Seven

They spent three days in Raleigh, but after the first one, Rand spent very little time in meetings. He invited Phoebe to accompany him to the one working dinner he had to attend and seemed to want her company as much as she wanted his.

Although they spent a great deal of their time together in bed, or on the floor, or up against a wall, Rand insisted on doing things with her besides making love. He said that being his woman did not mean spending twenty-four-seven in bed. Not that she would have minded. Making love with Rand was pure pleasure, but knowing he wanted more than sex with her gave her hope for a relationship beyond their one-week agreement.

On their last night in Raleigh, Rand took her to a small hole-in-the-corner restaurant located in a strip mall of all places. While the outside was unassuming, the interior was as elegant as any five-star restaurant she'd ever been to, and she quickly learned it was *the restaurant* for steak lovers in Raleigh. The waiter led them to a small table in the back room. She smiled as Rand pulled out her chair and helped her into her seat instead of allowing the waiter to do it.

"You're going to love the steak here, baby."

"And what would you do if it turned out I didn't care for steak at all?" she asked tongue-in-cheek.

He folded his tall form into the chair across from hers, his gray eyes full of humor and sexy lights. "Come on, honey. Not only do I know for a fact you love a good steak, I know you like it medium-well and prefer it topped with sautéed mushrooms when they're available."

"I guess you paid attention." For some reason, that really surprised her. It seemed like an intimate thing for someone to know about her, to care enough to notice.

"You'd be surprised at the things I pay attention to." His expression implied things that made her insides melt.

"I'm *surprised* you paid attention to that much."

"Why?" He looked genuinely puzzled. "We've spent enough time together over the last few years."

She laughed, though the sound was a little choked. "I'm not exactly the type of woman you notice, Rand."

His dark brows rose. "That's why we've had to buy so many condoms this week, because you're not the type of woman I notice."

Even after three days making love in every way she could imagine, and some she hadn't, she could still blush. And she did as her gaze skittered around the restaurant, trying to tell if anyone had heard him.

He laughed out loud, the masculine sound caressing her insides. "What's the matter, baby? Worried someone here is going to figure out we're sleeping together?"

She frowned at him. "No, but you don't need to announce it to the whole restaurant either."

His face moved into lines of mock solemnity, and it was at that moment that she realized just how frequently he had smiled and laughed over the last few days. Which in itself said something, because on a normal day, solemn described him best.

"I'll try to be more circumspect."

"Will you really?" She knew just what kind of circumspect he meant, and it wasn't anything like her usual unassuming, living in the background sort of circumspect.

He winked, looking roguish, confirming her suspicion.

Maybe a little of his own medicine would be just what the doctor ordered. She unobtrusively slipped her pump off her right foot, then lifted her stocking-clad foot to caress him under the cover of the long white tablecloth.

Just as her toes made contact with the familiar bulge in his pants, she said, "You do that very thing."

His body jerked, his gray eyes going dark with immediate desire, and his sex surged against her foot. "You little devil. You'll pay for that."

She rubbed her toes up and down his length, making sure her torso above the table did not move or in any way give away what she was doing under the table with her foot. "Will I?"

His eyes closed, and his head tilted back slightly.

She didn't say anything, but cuddled him with her foot, keeping up a light rubbing motion. They stayed that way for several seconds until his eyes slid open again. The look in them burned her from the inside out.

"I thought you were a shy little virgin."

She curled her toes forward and rejoiced in the feel of him jerking hard against her. "I was. Three days ago."

He shook his head, his jaw tight, his expression that of a man in pain. "I think you were a siren just waiting to be let out of her shell."

Did that mean he thought she would be this way with another man? She knew that she wouldn't be. If she had married Carter four years ago, she would *never* have discovered this side of herself. It would have been impossible because this wanton nature she'd never known she had was a direct result of being in close proximity to Rand.

Suddenly a warm hand closed over her foot, pressing her more firmly to him. She instinctively tried to pull back, but his grip was too tight.

"I'm tormenting myself with this." His voice, low and gravelly, sounded as though he meant it.

The waiter arrived, and she lost the opportunity to answer. Rand ordered for both of them, and she was glad because she didn't think her brain would have worked well enough to conjure up a dinner selection.

After pouring them each a glass of wine from a bottle he left on the table, their server left.

Rand's hand squeezed on her foot in a convulsive movement, and he looked like he was in pain.

She chewed on her lower lip. "I'm sorry. I didn't mean to hurt you."

His thumb caressed her arch, and she felt it straight to the core of her.

"This is one kind of pain I can live with."

She didn't reply. Couldn't reply. He was doing something to her foot that made pleasure arc through her insides and caused her nipples to tighten painfully.

"Do we have to eat?" Her voice broke on the last word as she had to swallow down a moan of delight.

He nodded, his head moving slowly while his eyes spoke a message to her that she could not mistake. "I want you to have plenty of energy later."

"Then you'd better let go of my foot," she choked out, feeling closer to orgasm than any woman should in the middle of a packed to capacity restaurant. "I don't think I can handle this kind of pleasure in public."

His hand moved in another mysterious way. "Are you sure?"

She couldn't stifle the moan this time, and even as the pleasure grew, her cheeks heated with embarrassment. "Yes."

His hand stilled. After a soothing caress, he let go.

A full minute passed before she had the wherewithal to move her foot. She slipped her shoe back on, her foot still tingling from his touch. "I guess I'm not up to your speed."

He winked and shifted imperceptibly in his seat. "Don't you believe it, baby. I've never come sitting at a table in a restaurant, but one more stroke from that sexy little foot of yours and I would have."

She tried to control her racing heart, but she loved knowing she affected him so strongly. The knowledge increased the intense desire shaking her insides. "Talk about something else," she pleaded.

"What would you like to talk about?"

Their future, but she wasn't about to bring that subject up. She wasn't ready to have her hopes dashed. "Why did you stay in New Hope after your mom died?" she asked with real curiosity.

It had to have been harder on him, and it wasn't as if he and his father had been close.

"Susan."

"Oh." She should have realized that.

He'd been dating Susan at the time, and they had been married within six months of his mother's death. Phoebe looked down at her fingers against the white tablecloth, seeing nothing interesting in her basic manicure, but not wanting to see the look of sadness she knew would be in his eyes. She could handle the fact that he had been married and that his wife had died.

What hurt Phoebe was the knowledge he'd buried his heart with the other woman.

He sighed, and she looked up at the sound.

"That's not all of it."

"It's not?"

"It's my hometown. I started my business there because I wanted to prove to all the people who had looked down at my mother for being a mistress and not a wife that I was every bit as good as they were."

"You succeeded."

"Did I?"

"How can you ask that? Your company is the biggest employer in New Hope."

"That doesn't stop your aunt from thinking you could do a lot better than me in the marriage stakes or Carter's mother from pretending I don't exist."

Just the thought of marriage with Rand was enough to stop Phoebe's breath in her throat.

Rand watched with interest as Phoebe averted her eyes, her cheeks a delicate pink. She fiddled with her spoon, turning it over and over on the tablecloth. "Mrs. Sloane has her own way of dealing with the past, and Aunt Emmaline has some pretty old-fashioned ideas."

"Is that what you call it?"

Those pretty hazel eyes met his, their depths soft with understanding. "What difference does it make? Aunt Emmaline and her friends aren't the great arbiters of New Hope's social conscience."

"Don't tell them that. It'll break their hearts."

Instead of laughing, or at least smiling, as he expected her to at his facetious comment, she gazed at him with a too serious expression. "I think you're an amazing man."

It was happening again, that warm feeling in the region of his heart. It had been occurring with more and more frequency each day he spent with Phoebe as his woman. He didn't like it because that kind of warmth was always followed by the coldness of loss.

"Thanks, honey, but I finally reached a point where I realized it didn't matter what anyone else thought. I'm the man I want to be."

"Are you?"

She'd just said she thought he was amazing; what was she getting at? "What are you asking?"

She swallowed, as though she was nervous, but one thing he'd come to know about his Phoebe was that she was no

"What a horrible thing to do. That's just plain wicked."

"I guess Carter thinks so, too," he found himself telling her when he'd had no intention of sharing his brother's nutty scheme with anyone. "He's got some crazy idea about giving me half of Sloane Electronics."

Phoebe's eyes grew wide. "So that's why he came home."

Rand didn't know. His brother made no bones about wanting the lithium on Luna Island for Sloane Electronics, but then he wanted to give half of the company to Rand. Or so he said.

"When did Carter tell you that?"

"He called." Actually, he'd called multiple times, but Rand hadn't picked up the subsequent calls on his cell.

"I'm glad."

"I don't trust people named Sloane."

Phoebe's eyes filled with understanding, going warm with compassion. "That's hardly a surprise after the way both your grandfather and dad behaved."

"The old man made damn sure Hoyt never married my mom."

"And Hoyt did nothing about it."

"That's for sure."

"That kind of pressure wouldn't have worked on a man like you. You would have told your grandfather to take a flying leap and built your own company."

Which was essentially what he had done.

"But your dad stayed in a marriage he didn't want for the sake of money and appearances. It's pretty obvious he never loved Carter's mother. A man doesn't have affairs when he loves his wife."

Rand tended to agree, no matter what current psychobabble stated. "He didn't love my mother either."

"No. He would have married her otherwise."

"Mom thought he did. She felt bad for him and accepted a shadowy place in his life until the day she died."

"You refused to stay in the shadows," Phoebe said perceptively, her grip on his wrist tightening momentarily.

"That's right. I gave him a choice, publicly acknowledge me or be publicly denied by me."

"He chose to acknowledge you."

And to this day, Rand didn't know if that was because he was afraid of the scandal Rand might have caused or because he'd wanted a real bond with his oldest son. But all he said was, "Yes."

"You aren't responsible for the choices of your father."

"I finally figured that out." About the time he married Susan, but then he'd lost her, and he'd come to accept that love had too high a price to pay.

His mother had paid dearly for her love of Hoyt Sloane. Rand had paid for that love throughout his childhood, too. Susan and their baby's death had been the final blow to a heart that turned to stone from the battering.

That night in bed, Phoebe curled into Rand's sleeping body and ached for the boy who had been denied so much and the man who had lost so much. She loved him with an unstoppable love, but after their discussion in the restaurant, she realized how little hope she had of him ever risking his heart on love again. It hurt, but she couldn't blame him. All he knew was the losing side of love, something she understood all too well. He wouldn't give her a lifetime, but she had three more days with him, and she would make the best of that time.

For now, she had him, and she was going to revel in that, not ruin what time she had left as his woman, grieving for what would not be.

If he did dismiss her from his life, she would have memories to warm her lonely bed.

Phoebe listened to the third message from Carter Sloane on her answering machine. They'd arrived back in New Hope in the early morning hours. Before going to his office, Rand had dropped her at her apartment so she could check on things. He expected her to be back at his place when he got home from the office, but it was not even late morning yet, and she had the whole day ahead of her without him.

She had wanted to cling when he had left, but she couldn't very well demand he take more time off from work just because their days together were over half gone.

Feeling depressed and trying really hard not to, she picked up the phone to dial Carter's number. He said he wanted to meet her for lunch to talk about Rand. She believed him. Apparently, Carter had realized he needed his brother, even if Rand hadn't reached that conclusion yet.

Two hours later, at a small downtown bistro, she weaved between the tables toward Carter. He stood up as she reached him and pulled out her chair.

She smoothed her short skirt under her and sat down. "Thanks."

"My pleasure. It looks like being with Rand has had a definite impact on your wardrobe."

Phoebe looked down at the strappy summer dress and smiled wryly. "You could say that."

"I like it."

"So does Rand."

"I'm glad." Carter's eyes probed hers. "Are you sure you know what you're doing, Phoebe? This new relationship thing between you and Rand is pretty coincidental to the discovery of lithium on Luna Island."

Apparently everyone assumed both she and Rand had been spouting off at the charity reception. Of course, when they stopped seeing each other after a week and Rand started mining operations on Luna Island, Mrs. Sloane, Aunt Emmaline and Carter would know the truth about the deal, or at least be able to guess at it. The thought bothered Phoebe, but there was nothing she could do about it.

"I didn't come here to discuss my relationship with Rand. I'm a grown-up and have to make my own decisions."

"And mistakes?" Carter asked gently.

"And mistakes, but then I've done that before."

He winced. "Point taken."

She softened toward him immediately. "I didn't mean it like that. I'm honestly grateful that you left like you did. Rand brings out things in me that I didn't even know were there."

Carter looked at her with eyes that saw into her soul. "Yes, I believe he does. I'm sorry I didn't."

"I thought I loved you." But the lukewarm feeling she'd had for Carter was nothing like the overwhelming passion and need she felt for Rand.

"For what it's worth, I cared about you, and I really didn't want to hurt you."

"Then why did you leave?" she asked with more curiosity than accusation.

"I found out stuff about my dad that sent me into a tailspin. It made me question things about myself and my commitment to you. Hoyt loved my mother when he married her, or at least thought he did, but he'd been having an affair right up until the wedding. Rand was born six months before I was."

"I know that."

"Mom never forgave him, but she refused a divorce, and my grandfather made sure Dad wouldn't push the issue."

"But he resumed his affair with Rand's mother."

"Yes. And said he loved her."

"I don't understand why that made you leave me." What did his father's tomcat ways have to do with Carter's plans to marry her?

"There was a woman."

"You were having an affair?" Now that shocked her. She couldn't imagine it of Carter.

"No." His face clenched. "But I wanted her, and I thought maybe I was as incapable of fidelity as my father. You deserved so much better than the life my mother led with Hoyt."

Compassion moved in Phoebe's heart for this incredible man who believed he had his father's emotional weakness. "You aren't your father, Carter. He put money and social position above love. You wouldn't do that."

"Are you sure about that?"

"Yes."

Carter sighed. "Maybe you're right, but I was right, too, that the emotional connection didn't last."

"You still care about me, or you wouldn't have been worried about Rand hurting me."

"That's not enough to base a marriage on."

"No doubt, but then you didn't make that mistake, did you?"

Carter looked at her, his expression unreadable. "I guess you could look at it that way, but I didn't ask you to lunch to discuss me."

She smiled. "I didn't think you had."

The waiter arrived and took their order, and she waited until he was gone before she spoke again.

"So why did you invite me to lunch? I should probably tell you up front I won't be negotiating for Luna Island. I promised it to Rand." Which was as good as telling Carter she'd made the deal with his brother.

Only Carter didn't look as though he'd made the connection because his expression didn't change. "I had that figured out. You're not going to sell mineral rights to me when your lover wants them, too."

Her lover. *For a week.* And she wanted so much more, was desperately hoping for so much more. "So . . ."

"I wanted to talk about Rand."

"Did you come back to make peace with him?"

"He's my brother. It's time we lived like it."

"I agree, but I'm sure your mother doesn't."

"She made her own choices, and I'm making mine."

Phoebe nodded. Mrs. Sloane had opted to kick her husband out of her bed, but insisted on staying married to him. She had been cold to Carter, obviously blaming him in some way for his father's sins. While Phoebe felt a certain amount of compassion for the older woman, she couldn't help being bothered by the price both Rand and Carter had paid for her stubborn inability to see any viewpoint but her own.

"I was hoping you'd convince Rand to talk to me."

"I thought you'd already talked. He told me you wanted to sign over part of the company to him."

"I'm surprised he told you. He wasn't very open to the idea, and he hasn't taken any of my calls since that one."

"Rand's a proud man. He doesn't need your company."

"I know, but I need to right the wrongs of the past. He's my older brother. He should have inherited along with me. We're family and that should mean something."

"I agree."

"So you'll get him to talk to me?"

"You think I have that kind of influence with him?"

"You're his lover. I've seen how he looks at you. I thought he was going to take a swing at me at the charity reception. Yes, I think he'll listen to you."

It was a heady concept. "I'll try."

"Thanks." The expression in Carter's eyes reflected two things: relief and frustration that he'd had to ask for her help.

He and his brother had a lot in common. Rand's pride would have balked at asking for help, too.

"You had lunch with my damn brother?"

Phoebe jumped, shocked by the incandescent rage that had erupted out of nowhere when she told Rand that Carter wanted to talk to him. No, that wasn't quite right. The fury had come when Rand realized she'd had lunch with Carter.

"Yes. I don't see what the big deal is."

Rand's eyes narrowed to angry slits, his big body vibrating with an anger she would never have thought she could ignite. "That's precisely it. Our deal."

Tension seeped into her at the mention of their arrangement. "What do you mean?"

"You wanted one week in my bed as my woman."

Pain contracted her heart with viselike intensity. He *was* still thinking in terms of a one-week time limit. She hadn't expected anything different, but oh, she had hoped. Even if he couldn't love her, they could have maintained their relationship, but apparently Rand didn't want to.

"So?" was all she could force past the lump of emotion in her throat.

"My woman doesn't have lunch with my damn brother."

"Stop calling him that. He's not damned."

Rand stepped forward until he was towering over her with intimidating ferocity. "He's not your fiancé anymore either. If you belong to me, you stay away from him."

She swallowed nervously, but refused to back down. This was too important. Rand needed Carter, even if he didn't realize it, or was just too stubborn and proud to admit it. Besides, his anger was probably because he thought she was considering reneging on the deal that was now ripping her heart to shreds.

"I promised you the deed to Luna Island. I don't break my promises, and you don't have to worry I'm going to sell it to Carter."

Rand's big hands cupped her shoulders. Despite the fury on his face, the hold was gentle. "This isn't about the island."

"Then what is it about?" she choked out, finding it difficult to talk as she always did when in such close proximity to the man she loved.

"You having lunch with Carter." He said his brother's name like it was a curse.

"He's not your enemy, Rand."

"He sure as hell isn't my friend."

She licked lips, gone dry from stress. "He's your brother, and he *could* be your friend. If you'd let him."

"Is that what he told you? He wants to be my *friend?* This isn't Mister Rogers' neighborhood, Phoebe. Carter's a businessman, and the only interest he has in me is your promise to give me the deed to an island rich with lithium."

She shook her head, trying to stay focused on the conversation when all she wanted was the oblivion of Rand's arms. Only it was a temporary oblivion, and she now knew beyond the shadow of a doubt that it was also a false oblivion. There was nothing between them but sex. There couldn't be and he still be so focused on the terms of their deal.

"That's not true. He wants to talk to you. Is that really so much to ask?"

Rand's big body moved closer to hers, his expression changing from anger to something else. "I'll think about it, *but you stay away from him.*"

She'd about had it with his bossiness. "You can't dictate who I talk to."

"Our deal says I can," he bit out, the anger returning in a flash.

"I don't think—"

"If you want to have lunch with him in three days' time," he said, his words overriding hers, "hell, if you want to have sex with him, I'll have nothing to say about it, but until then, you're *my woman.*"

She couldn't believe he'd said that. Did he really not care if she went from his bed to Carter's? She shook her head in denial of that truth.

Rand's expression turned feral. "In your own words, Phoebe, *a deal is a deal.* Are you going to stick by the terms, or not?"

Right now all she wanted was to curl up in a hole and cry her heart out. She didn't care about the deal's terms. She didn't even care if Rand and Carter ever found their way to being a family. She just wanted to get away.

She yanked herself from his loose hold and stumbled backward.

She'd been an idiot to think for even a second that a real relationship could evolve from a week of uncommitted sex. Oh, damn it! She was not going to cry. Not in front of him.

She gritted her teeth against the sobs that wanted to tear out of her throat and spun on her heel, heading toward the bedroom. She started throwing clothes into her suitcase even as Rand came storming into the room after her.

"What the hell are you doing?"

She wasn't answering such a stupid question.

He grabbed the suitcase and yanked it out of her reach. "We still have three days left."

She spun to face him. "Don't worry, I'll see my lawyer in the morning. You'll get your deed, but this part of the deal is over." She swept her hand in an arc that encompassed the bed and the rest of the room where she'd given him her virginity and he'd given her so much pleasure.

Rand went gray. "You want to go to Carter now?"

"I don't want to go to Carter at all! But I don't want to stay with you either." The words hurt her to say, but only a true masochist would continue building memories that would torment her in the empty loneliness to come, she now realized.

"You wanted a week with me."

"I changed my mind."

"Because I won't talk to Carter?" Rand's hands fisted at his sides. "If it's that important to you, I'll talk to him, all right?"

He acted as though he really cared if she left early, but she couldn't let herself be deceived by her hopes again.

"I truly hope you'll give Carter a chance to be your brother, but I can't stay here anymore." She lost her battle with the tears, and they spilled over, burning a path down her cheeks. She reached for the suitcase. "I've got to go."

Strong fingers peeled hers away from the suitcase and sent it tumbling to the floor. Then familiar arms wrapped around her, his face nuzzling into hers. "I can't let you go, baby."

She turned her face from his kisses. "I can't stay for three more days." But he was making it almost impossible to leave.

The insistent peal of the bell broke through the carnage going on between her and Rand. "You'd better get that."

"No. We need to talk. Whoever it is can go away."

"It might be Carter."

"If it is, the doorman knows better than to key up to the penthouse level again."

But the ding of the elevator coming from the other room indicated the doorman had done just that. "Maybe a different one is on duty."

From the expression on Rand's face, she was glad she wasn't the hapless soul in the lobby, no matter who it was. In fact, she could feel gratitude not to be in Carter's shoes at the moment. Rand looked ready to commit murder.

He turned to go, but stopped at the door. "No more packing. You aren't going anywhere."

Her heart split a little wider. "I have to."

"No. We have to talk."

"What good will it do?"

"Carter left you standing practically at the altar, but you had lunch with him, don't I even deserve a half an hour of your time to sort out our relationship?"

They didn't have a relationship, and he'd made that very obvious, but she couldn't deny him. "I won't leave just yet."

He nodded and left.

She considered following him, but wasn't sure if her presence would be better or worse for the two brothers to speak. Only the voice she heard coming from the living room was not Carter's deep tones, but the high-pitched tones of a very angry woman.

"How dare you insinuate yourself into my son's life?" Cassandra Sloane's freezing question hung in the air between them as Phoebe came careening into the living room.

"Mrs. Sloane, what are you doing here?"

The distaste that came across the old biddy's features was enough to send what was left of Rand's patience packing. "I don't know what she's doing here, but she's just about to leave."

"I am not leaving until you promise me you won't steal your brother's birthright!"

The sound of his father's wife yelling was enough to shock Rand speechless.

Not so Phoebe. "Rand isn't trying to steal anything. Carter wants him to have part of the company because they're brothers and your husband should have left it to both of them to begin with."

A look of bitter satisfaction filled Cassandra Sloane's eyes. "He couldn't. His father saw to that, and it was only right. A man's mistress doesn't inherit, nor does her illegitimate son."

"Rand is Hoyt's son, too!"

"Yes, he is. He's also my brother, and this has nothing to do with you, Mother."

Rand hadn't heard the elevator ding again, but his brother was there, glaring at his mother.

She turned on Carter, her mouth twisted like a prune. "You dare say that to me? Your father may not have left me anything, but it is your responsibility to support me off of the income from Sloane Electronics."

"I can support you off of half the company just fine."

"You're being stupidly sentimental. This man has no place in your life. He never has had."

"He does now." Carter met Rand's eyes. "If you want one, that is."

"Of course he does." It was Phoebe's turn to step in apparently.

"Stay out of this, young lady. It's none of your concern."

"I care about both Rand and Carter; that makes it my concern."

If she cared so much about him, why the hell was she leaving him three days early?

"Mother, the only person here who has nothing to add, is you."

"Oh, really? You think I have nothing to add?" Mrs. Sloane's tone was one shade shy of total hysteria.

Rand didn't care what Mrs. Sloane had to add. He didn't think she would be so angry if Carter didn't mean what he'd said, which indicated he really did want a relationship with Rand. However, right now was not when Rand wanted to get into that. He was facing Phoebe walking out on him.

"Look, if you really want to give me part of your company, we can talk about it later, but right now is not a good time."

"You will discuss it with me, though?" Carter asked, hope burning in eyes that mirrored Rand's in shape and expression.

"Yes."

"If you're so set on giving away your inheritance, why don't you find your younger brother and give him part of the company, too?" she demanded, rage riding her hard.

"Younger brother?" Carter asked, his voice faint.

"Yes!" She turned to glare at Rand. "You thought your father loved your mother? Not likely. Hoyt Sloane didn't love anyone but himself. He had affairs, and one of them bore fruit."

"I've got another brother?" Carter demanded.

"Yes, and I suppose you're going to want to give him part of the company, too!"

"Sounds good to me."

Mrs. Sloane looked ready to have an apoplectic fit. "You're insane."

"Maybe, but unfortunately for you, I'm not certifiable, and Sloane Electronics belongs to me."

Mrs. Sloane didn't bother to answer but swung on her heel and headed to the elevator.

Carter looked at Rand. "Have lunch with me tomorrow. It looks like we've got more to discuss than the company."

So many emotions were swirling through Rand, he wasn't sure what to do with any of them, but his brother was right. They did need to talk. "Yes."

Carter followed his mother, slipping into the elevator with an expression that said he was going to get to the bottom of the bomb his mother had dropped on them all.

When Rand turned back from watching his brother leave, Phoebe had gone back into the bedroom.

A strong hand closed over hers on the suitcase. "I thought we agreed no more packing."

"What's the use of me staying?" she asked him, her emotions still too close to the surface to meet his gaze.

"I need you."

The words would have been all she wanted to hear just an hour ago, but now she knew they meant something very different than what she needed them to mean. "I can't be a body in your bed anymore. I don't know why I ever thought I could."

He spun her to face him, his expression fierce. "How can you believe that?"

She swiped at tears that had started the minute she'd begun packing again. "How can I believe anything else when you tell me you don't care if I go to Carter's bed in three days' time?"

His body went completely motionless, and if his complexion had been gray earlier, it was pasty now. "I don't want you to go to Carter at all."

She took a deep breath, but it shuddered out again on tears she couldn't seem to stem. "You don't care who I sleep with when you're done with me."

"Done with you?" he asked hoarsely. His face spasmed with some internal pain. "I'll never be *done* with you."

She stared at him, entranced by the emotion burning in his gray eyes.

He swallowed convulsively, suspicious moisture making those eyes seem darker than they were. "I thought my heart was rock-solid, but you taught me I can still bleed. If you leave me, I'm going to hemorrhage."

"I don't want to go. I love you," she admitted, knowing only that she had to tell him, at least once.

His arms tightened, and she found herself wrapped up against him as close as two bodies could get without making love. "I loved Susan."

"I know."

"It hurt to lose her and our son, more than I thought I could ever hurt, but when you threatened to walk out, I took a body blow that felt like it was going to kill me. When Mrs. Sloane and Carter showed up, all I could think of was getting rid of them so I could work things out with you."

Was he saying he loved her? His heart was beating fast against her ear. Was it a heart that had turned from stone to living, pulsing flesh?

"But the deal . . ." It had been all that mattered a few minutes ago.

"I want new terms for our deal."

She pulled away, blinking back the tears and trying to see

CARTER'S STORY

Chapter One

Anticipation thrummed through Carter Sloane's body.

Soon he would know the answer to a very important question, a question that had been plaguing him for over four years.

Would Daisy Jackson's lips taste as good as they looked?

Impatiently, he increased his pace as he approached her office. The building was pretty much deserted, and he'd made sure it was so. He'd even sent security off the floor. He didn't want any witnesses for what he was hoping would take place. A kiss that would prove the desire went both ways.

Sweat broke out at his temples, and he tugged at the collar of his custom-tailored shirt that suddenly felt too tight. Thinking about Daisy made his blood so hot, it boiled in his veins.

His torment had been working for Sloane Electronics since she was eighteen. Not that he'd met her that early on. If he had, he wondered if he would ever have ended up engaged to Phoebe. Starting in clerical, Daisy had worked her way to an important behind-the-scenes position in marketing.

She was much too shy to thrive on the sales team, or even in a position where she had to present her ideas to upper management. He found that endearing.

He'd met her over four years ago when she'd first moved into the marketing department, and he had fallen in instant lust. She was the main reason he'd left Phoebe practically standing at the altar. If he could feel such strong sexual attraction to another woman, he had no business marrying Phoebe. He had been convinced he carried his father's curse when it came to relationships and women.

But four long years of wanting the same woman, dreaming about her and finally getting to the point where he wasn't even interested in sex with other women, had taught him something about himself.

He had a helluva lot more staying power than his father. He might not be any more capable of real love, but he *could* do the fidelity thing.

Now he just had to convince Daisy she wanted to do it with him.

He was almost positive that her hormones were as affected as his. She blushed when their eyes met, and whenever he came close, her breathing got erratic. All definite signs the attraction was mutual, but he had to find out for sure.

Right now. He couldn't wait any longer.

It was after six P.M., but he knew she'd still be in her office. She had no social life. He'd asked around and discovered she never dated. Which shocked the hell out of him. Were the men around her blind or just stupid? His little Daisy was ripe for the plucking, and he was the lucky guy who was going to savor her sweet fruit.

He stepped into her office, and sure enough she was busy typing away at the computer. His nostrils flared just like an animal in heat scenting his mate as her vanilla perfume reached out and surrounded him.

"Don't you ever go home?"

She jumped and spun her chair around to face him.

Her black hair flew like a silk cloud around her face, and

her almond-shaped brown eyes went wide like a Japanese animated cartoon. *"Mr. Sloane."*

He took a step farther into the room and noticed with interest how she scooted back in her chair, even though the desk was an effective barrier between them. "Call me Carter."

He couldn't picture himself coming inside her as she screamed *Mr. Sloane* in his ear.

"I-I don't feel comfortable calling the owner of the company by his first name."

He watched her luscious lips move and form the words. Their natural raspberry fullness just begged to be kissed. Why didn't other men react to the sensuality she exuded? Her lack of a social life was inexplicable to him, even taking into account her shyness. But he'd been in the room when she was exuding subtle mating signals, of which he was sure she was oblivious, and so were the men working with her.

He'd noticed, though, and they made him nuts.

She made a nervous movement with her hands as his silence stretched, and his libido went into attack-and-conquer mode. It had been way too long. If his experiment failed, he didn't know what he was going to do.

It could not fail.

She had to want him, too.

No way could this much desire be one-sided.

"I'm the owner, aren't I?"

She nodded, her pink tongue darting out to lick her lips and then retreating in a game of erotic peek-a-boo he was positive she did not intend, and he had to stifle a groan.

"I don't mind you calling me Carter. In fact, I prefer it."

"But . . ."

"Daisy, even your admin calls me Carter. I think you're the only person in the company besides old Mrs. Berger in the cafeteria that calls me Mr. Sloane."

She sighed, as if it really mattered. "All right . . . Carter."

He didn't know why, but he felt like he'd won a major concession. "Good. Now, I have a question for you."

She sat up straighter, scooting her chair forward, and clasped her hands on top of her desk. "Yes?"

"Have you ever felt sexually harassed here?"

Her dark brown eyes opened wide, and her lips parted, but nothing came out, not even a huff of air.

She was taking so long to answer, he was beginning to wonder if there was some guy working for him that he was going to have to fire. "Have you?"

Finally, she shook her head. "Uh . . . no."

"Good."

She knocked some papers off her desk and bent to pick them up, sending a CD-ROM in its case flying to the floor as well. She gathered the papers and dropped them in an untidy heap on her desk with the CD-ROM on top. Her cheeks were now as berry pink as her lips.

"Mr. Slo—I mean, Carter, why did you ask me that?"

He moved around her desk, stalking her and hoping like hell her nerves were due to reciprocal attraction to the boss and not fear. "It's important."

She leaned back in her chair, away from him. "But why?"

"If you don't want to do anything, you don't have to."

"That's good." She was looking at him as though he'd gone nuts, and the truth was, he had.

His nuts were controlling his brain, and it wasn't doing his powers of conversation any good. While he could schmooze company presidents, man-woman communication was not his thing, and right now he felt like a rookie manager giving his first presentation to the board of directors.

He gave up on the subtle approach and decided on blunt honesty. "Daisy, I want to kiss you, but I don't want you to feel pressured into letting me because I own the company you work for."

She squeaked like a startled mouse, and then shook her head, sending that gorgeous black silk cloud into motion again. Disappointment took his heart in its grip and squeezed. Had he been wrong about her reaction to him? Or was she afraid of it, and how far could he push it without going into the realms of harassment? Not very damned far.

She gaped at him. "*What?*"

He took another step toward her, finding it more and more difficult to rein in the primitive urges she brought out in him. "I want to kiss you."

"Now?"

That was definitely better than *no*. "Yes."

"I-I . . ."

He forced down the desire to just pick her right up out of that small black office chair and devour her lips. "You don't have to let me if you don't want to. Your job is not on the line. I won't hold it against you if you say no." But his balls were going to turn blue and fall off if that happened.

"I promise," he said for good measure. This had to be absolutely voluntary on her part, or it wasn't happening.

She tucked her shiny black hair behind one ear in a nervous gesture. It rippled over her shoulder, and he wanted to touch it. *Bad.*

"You really want to kiss me?"

"Yes."

"Now?" she repeated, and it was all he could do not to shout the affirmative.

"Yes, now." His voice came out like some kind of animal growl, and he hoped like Hades he hadn't scared her.

She stood up and closed all but two feet of the distance left between them.

He had long arms, and they were itching to reach out so he could grab her. It took more concentration than he felt he could spare to stop from doing it.

"My job doesn't depend on this?"

"No." More growling. In a minute he was going to start howling like a wolf at a full moon.

Moons made him think of backsides, naked backsides. Carter came closer to losing it than he had since he was fifteen and necking with his girlfriend when she let him cop a feel under her blouse for the first time.

"Is that why you asked me about the um . . . the sexual harassment thing? Did you think I felt pressured sexually by you?"

"Not yet." He hadn't pressured her at all. He'd been extremely careful not to.

"But now you want to kiss me." She seemed to be having a really hard time taking it in.

He closed the distance between them and laid his hands on her shoulders. Her small bones felt fragile under his fingers. "I want to kiss you, and I need you to either say yes or tell me to take a hike in something like two seconds."

Her head tilted back so she could see him. She didn't look scared. She didn't look intimidated. She just looked confused, and at that very moment that wasn't a whole lot better than the other two. He needed to have his lips on hers in the worst way.

"Do you want to use your tongue?" She asked it like she'd ask if he wanted a mint, and it took him a second to grasp the meaning of the words.

When he did, his knees about buckled. "Yes. I'm going to want to use my tongue."

She bit her lip and stared at him for a second. "Oh."

"Is that a problem?"

"I don't like using tongues."

It was his turn to stare. Not like tongues? No. She couldn't possibly have said that. He wanted to use his tongue in a lot more places than her mouth.

"I'll make you like it."

"If I don't, will you stop?"

"Stop kissing you?"

"Stop putting your tongue in my mouth."

His knees did buckle, and he pivoted to fall back against her desk. He leaned on the edge and pulled her between his legs, so her body was one inch from rubbing up against the biggest, baddest erection he'd ever had.

"I'll stop if you don't like it."

"How will you know? I can't talk with—"

He couldn't bear to hear her say it again. "Hit my shoulder. I'll stop if you hit my shoulder."

"Okay."

His hands gripped convulsively on her shoulders. "Did you just say I could kiss you?"

"Only if you stop using your tongue if I tap your shoulder."

"I promise." But he was going to do everything in his power to make her like it.

She clasped her hands in front of her, closed her eyes, lifted her face and pursed her lips as though she'd just taken a bite out of a crab apple.

He didn't laugh. He couldn't. His sex hurt too much, but man, it was funny.

Hadn't she ever been soul-kissed, or didn't she think he could do it? Either way, she was in for a shock.

He lowered his head and stopped to savor her scent. Vanilla and pheromones mixed together in a cocktail that went straight to his head and not the one attached to his neck. He kissed her once, softly, and savored the feel of lips he'd been wanting for four interminable years. Then he broke contact and waited with his mouth poised just above her own.

Two seconds went by. Three. Four. Five. Her eyes opened and looked straight into his. The disappointment there was food for his starving libido.

"Is that all?"

He closed his mouth over hers before she finished speaking, catching her lips apart. He kissed her with all the finesse twenty-nine years of living had given him.

Her lips were soft and so sweet, he would gladly eat them every night after dinner for dessert. Heck, he'd be happy to have them instead of dinner. Anything so he could have *her*.

He wasn't rough, but it took all his self-control and then some to be gentle, to coax her into accepting the kind of kiss he needed to give her. He nibbled at her lower lip, tasting it with the tip of his tongue. She let her mouth open a little bit farther, and he dipped inside, feeling as if he was on an overdose of pleasure as her honey-sweet taste lured him in farther. He was careful not to dominate her mouth, though. Not yet. He wanted to lure her into seeking more.

He did a series of dip and retreat moves that had him shaking with the effort it took to let her set the pace. But finally, her tongue came in search of his. She slid it along his, inviting him back into her mouth with shy enthusiasm and very little skill.

He let her have her way.

She moaned and arched into him. He cupped that incredible backside he wanted so desperately to see naked with one big hand and pressed her forward. It brought her mound into direct contact with his rock-hard and aching penis.

He could feel pre-ejaculate wet his tip, and he lifted her, using her body to caress his needy flesh. All the while, he knew he was taking it too far. This wasn't the time or the place. He knew the passion was mutual. They could pursue it later. However, none of the arguments could put a hand brake on the need that had been building up for four years.

Worse for his self-control, she was as lost to the pleasure as he was. She writhed against him, her fingers locked like manacles around his neck.

He was so close to orgasm, he could feel the tingling at the base of his shaft.

He used the hand not busy grabbing her butt to feel her up in front. Her shirt was thin cotton, her bra couldn't be padded, not and him feel that hard and tight little peak poking the center of his palm. He squeezed her breast, kneaded it and then rubbed his palm over her nipple until she was climbing his legs, practically straddling him.

One shift of his big body and she *was* straddling him. He slipped his hand down over the resilient flesh of one of her cheeks, until his fingers were pressing into the apex of her thighs. Her panties were no barrier to him feeling the wetness their kiss had wrought between her legs.

Man, was she hot.

Hot and sexy and so on the edge that he wondered which one of them was going to go over first. Since it was both of them, he didn't even try to stop it. He'd wanted her too long to worry about the embarrassment of coming in his shorts like a horny adolescent.

He slipped his hand inside her panties. Skin so soft, it begged, for one caress after another quivered under his knowing hand. Pressing inexorably downward, he slid his middle finger into the slick and swollen warmth between her legs. Then he started undoing buttons with his other hand and got inside her shirt.

He'd been right. Her bra was some kind of thin, silky material, and it had a front clasp. With the flick of his wrist he had the catch open and was peeling fabric away from his prize, all the while kissing her with hunger built up by prolonged abstinence and fantasizing run amok.

One perfectly shaped mound was enough to fill his big hand. He squeezed and she moaned. He upbraided her nipple with his palm, and she made a deep animal sound in the back of her throat and started rubbing herself against him like a woman on a mission. He bucked against her, increasing the friction of their bodies while his tongue started to mock what his body so desperately wanted to do to her.

Wild desire raged out of control in his body, and he took

her nipple between his thumb and forefinger and gently pinched, then pulled it, rolling the sweet morsel between his fingers, before lightly pinching it again.

She exploded, her body bowing, pressing her swollen lips even harder against his throbbing erection, squeezing his finger in rhythmic contractions of her inner muscles.

Her mouth tore from his, and the guttural cry that erupted from her throat sent him into oblivion.

It lasted until stars danced on his closed eyelids and his body had shuddered over and over again in the longest climax he'd ever experienced. When it stopped, he was practically lying on her desk with her on top of him.

Her head landed against his shoulder like a dead weight, her body went boneless against him and he had to hold on to her so she wouldn't fall. Which was no mean feat considering how totally wasted he felt.

She mumbled something against his neck.

"What?" he wheezed, still breathing heavy from the best climax he'd had in ages.

Hell, maybe forever and *he hadn't even been inside her.*

"I like your tongue."

He couldn't help it. He laughed.

She giggled, and it was such a sweet sound, he hugged her.

"I think this is going to work."

"Kissing me? I'd say it already has."

"That, too."

Relief and more anticipation than he'd even been feeling before poured through him. It was all going to be okay.

"What is going to be okay?" she asked just as he realized he'd said it out loud.

"Us. Getting married."

Chapter Two

Daisy's entire body went rigid as Carter's words penetrated the sensual fog that had taken over her brain within seconds of his lips touching hers.

Maybe she was still fogged.

That would explain the hallucinations.

Carter Sloane talking about marriage to her, Daisy Jackson, had to be a delusion.

Even more so than the totally sexy owner of the company she worked for wanting to kiss her.

She had to wonder, had the whole darn thing been a fantasy? Was she dreaming? She'd had enough of them about Carter Sloane since coming to work for Sloane Electronics ten years ago.

None of her fantasies had had as much solid realism as the six-foot three-inch, two-hundred-pound body beneath her. His heart pounded against her chest. Had her dreams ever had so much detail before? She knew he'd climaxed. Her ears were ringing from his shout, but there was an awful lot of him left pressed against her feminine flesh.

Even in her sexiest fantasies, she hadn't envisioned quite that level of magnificent male presence.

Okay, definitely no fantasy, but the other . . .

She could not convince herself that he'd said the other. It would be too out of this world. Too extraordinary, and remarkable things like that did not happen in her humdrum life.

So, not only had she gone completely over the edge from a simple kiss, but she was definitely hallucinating.

Not good, Daisy.

She was twenty-eight years old, and she could count on one hand the number of times she'd climaxed while making love. *She wouldn't even have to use all her fingers.* And here she had gone and had the most mind blowing orgasm of them all from a kiss! Okay, maybe more than a kiss, with his finger still inside her.

Oh, gracious.

His finger was still inside her. And it felt good. Wonderful. Magnificent even. She wanted to move against that finger and experience a small taste of the pleasure he'd just given her. While he was probably lying there wondering how to get her off of him. *How embarrassing.*

She couldn't stay draped over Carter like a sack of potatoes. She had to get up, but how did she politely ask a man to stop playing with parts of her body she hadn't mentioned in public since tenth grade sex education class?

"Um, Carter?"

"Hmmm?" His chest rumbled with the sound against her bare breasts, and a new worry assailed her.

How was she going to cover up and get off him at the same time?

"I . . . Could you . . . Do you think you could move your hand?" she finally spit out.

"Sure."

She sighed with real relief. That had been a lot easier than she'd thought it was going to be.

He moved the hand that still held her in-no-way-rel:
nipple between two fingers so that it cupped her breas
stead. Then he sighed, too, as if he liked the position.

She knew she did, but she bet she was getting heavy.
wasn't some tiny thing like his former fiancée. They were
same height, but there the comparison ended. She was
where Phoebe was light, and Daisy's female attributes co
best be described as generous.

Carter didn't seem to mind, not with his hand cupping
of her boobs as if it was the most natural thing in the wo
to do, but maybe he was just being polite.

He was breathing too hard to be comfortable.

If she released her hold on him, he'd probably get the h
that he could let her go without hurting her feelings. Pull
her hands from around his neck, she pressed on his chest, l
instead of him releasing her, she ended up propped abo
him, her lower body just as close to his as it ever had been

His blue eyes were smoky with what she figured was sat
fied lust. She liked that because she was responsible. It wa:
very novel experience.

His mouth curved up at one corner in a smile she cou
only describe as smug, and he winked at her. "We're dyn
mite together."

He sounded really happy about that.

She couldn't imagine why, unless it was just the kiss-an
conquer male hormone showing itself. Their apparent sexu
compatibility was unlikely to impact either of their futures.

Darn it.

She frowned in concentration, trying not to react to th
feel of him touching her so intimately. "Carter, I really nee
you to move your hand."

"I did."

"Your other hand."

"This one?" And he moved it all right, backward and for

ward, bringing forth an involuntary reaction from her body, making her arch and go stiff and then shiver from the soles of her feet to the top of her head.

Oh, goodness!

She collapsed on top of him, her nose buried in his chest.

"I want to get off." She mumbled the blatant lie into his shirt.

"I'll get you off, honey. Just give me a sec." And he proceeded to show her just how easy it would be as his hand did insidious things to her unmentionable places.

She loved it, but she wasn't as lost to her body's insistent needs as she'd been a few minutes before. For instance, it occurred to her that the door to her office was wide open and anyone could walk in and see them like this. It wouldn't be so bad for Carter; he was on the bottom.

But she was on top, and security might think she'd gone crazy and attacked him in a lustful frenzy.

Sure.

Right.

Whatever. Right now embarrassment and fear at the possibility of getting caught definitely overruled desire.

Only he didn't seem to realize that at all. One more dangerous caress from that amazing finger and she was going to forget her manners and good sense all over again.

She couldn't think of what to do, so she hit his shoulder.

His hand stopped moving, and relief warred with disappointment inside her. "What was that for?"

"You said if I hit your shoulder, you'd stop."

His body stilled completely. "You want me to stop."

No. She wanted him to keep going. All night long. She wanted to have one of those nights she'd read about in romance novels, but that wasn't going to happen. She didn't know why he'd kissed her, but she couldn't believe he wanted her, not really.

There had to be some sort of logical explanation for what had just happened.

So, she lied. Again. It was getting to be a habit. He was a bad influence on her. "Yes. And I want to get off *of you.*"

His hand seemed to convulse in a possessive move that made her feel connected to him in a really frightening way. As if all this had been real and not just some sort of freaky aberration in her otherwise unexciting life.

"I want to kiss you again."

She lifted up in panic. "No."

He frowned. "Why not? I made you like my tongue."

Heat scorched up her body, and she knew her cheeks weren't the only things blushing. "Yes, you did, but you also said I had a choice, and I choose to stop now."

He closed his eyes and made a sound as though he was in pain, but his hand moved. Actually they both did, falling away from her body to lie like sleeping tigers on her desk. In her mind, they were that dangerous. She eyed them, flicking her gaze from one to the other with distrust, but he remained still.

"If you're going, go. I don't think I can keep my hands off you for much longer." His voice was tight with strain, and both hands curled into fists.

She believed him.

Scrambling off of him, she hoped he wouldn't open his eyes until she was covered up.

He didn't move, nor did his eyes open, and she spun away to refasten her bra and button up her shirt with her back to him.

"One day soon, I'm going to see every pale peach inch of you."

She started at the sound of his voice and whirled back to face him. He was leaning against the desk again, his hair mussed, his expression downright feral.

Who would have thought the elegant, sophisticated owner of Sloane Electronics could look so primitive?

She didn't know what to say, but an atavistic shudder shook her. Even as she reacted to that look on the most basic level, she was appalled with herself and horribly embarrassed by the way she had reacted to a simple kiss and some light petting.

It just went to show that six years without sex had left her extremely vulnerable.

"I'm sorry."

"What the hell for?"

"I sort of went crazy, and all you wanted to do was kiss me."

"Didn't you notice me going a little crazy, too?" He ran his fingers through dark brown hair. "If anyone should apologize, it should be me, but I'm not sorry."

"Why aren't you? All you wanted was a kiss, and we practically made love on top of my desk."

His eyelids lowered, and the expression on his face was nothing short of predatory. "We were a long way from making love, but I'd be happy to demonstrate the difference."

She backed up a step, even though he hadn't moved. "That's not a good idea."

"Married people have sex, honey. Or didn't you know?"

He was teasing her, but she didn't feel like laughing. "I know. I've been married, after all."

And she'd failed spectacularly at it, particularly the sex part. Of course, it hadn't helped that her husband had been a closet drug addict who had wanted a second income to support his habit more than he'd wanted a plain Jane wife.

Carter jerked as if startled. "Your personnel record doesn't show that."

She glared at him. "You've been reading my personnel file?"

"I own the company." He didn't look in the least repentant for invading her privacy like that. "I'm allowed."

She crossed her arms over her chest and sucked in a breath at the friction against her still aroused nipples. "That remains to be seen."

His smile was so sexy, it was lethal, but then it faded, and he was frowning again. "When were you married?"

"I got married when I was twenty."

"It doesn't say anything about it in your file."

"I never included him on my insurance or anything, so there's no reason why it should."

"When did you divorce?"

"We didn't."

She watched, fascinated, as all the color drained from Carter's face. *You're married?*

"My husband died on our second anniversary." He'd overdosed on heroin while at a party with his drug-using friends.

He'd forgotten it was their anniversary, or more likely simply hadn't cared. Anyway, he hadn't been with her, and after two years married to a man whose moods were drug induced, she hadn't minded at all.

His death had been sad, but she hadn't grieved like a woman in love should.

"I'm sorry." Carter looked as though he really meant it.

She shrugged. "I am, too. He was too young to die like he did."

Carter didn't look much better than he had a minute before. "Are you still grieving for him?"

"No."

Her marriage had been a mistake, but she would have tried to make it work, tried to get Jack help.

She hadn't gotten the chance. End of story.

Carter's smile was back in full force, and she about staggered under the impact.

"So, you're totally free to marry me."

The room grew black around the edges, and she stumbled backward until she fell into a chair beside the door to her office. "*What?*"

"I'm being pretty abrupt about this, aren't I?" Carter tugged at his tie until it was loose enough to pull off over his head. Then he unbuttoned the top two buttons on his dress shirt, and she wanted to ask him to undo more.

She stomped on the urge and simply nodded in answer to his question. She'd say abrupt about covered it.

He sighed and ran his long fingers through his hair again. "I'm sorry."

"That's okay." Her voice was faint, but at least it worked.

Which was a miracle when she considered all she'd been through in the last half hour.

Carter adjusted himself just like some jock teenager and then grimaced. "Look, honey, we need to talk, but I've got to take a shower. I'm a mess."

He indicated the front of his suit pants that couldn't hide the wet spot, despite their dark color.

She blushed and hastily looked away.

He laughed. "You're a case, you know that?"

She shrugged, suddenly realizing she wasn't all that comfortable between her legs herself.

She looked back at him, keeping her gaze strictly on his face this time. "I guess I could use a shower, too."

"Want to share?" he asked with a lot more seriousness than she could handle.

"No." Was that Minnie Mouse voice hers? She never squeaked. She wasn't the type.

Pragmatic. Practical. Plain. The three *p*s that described her perfectly. Another *p*.

"Are you sure about that?" The sensual promise in his

voice made her insides melt, but she kept a stiff upper lip and shook her head.

"Okay. Get your stuff and I'll drive you home."

"I have my car."

"I don't. Mine is in the shop."

"You need a ride home?" she asked.

Is that why he'd come to her office? No. He'd said he wanted to kiss her. She was pretty sure most men didn't feel the need to pay for a ride home with a kiss, even ones as sexy as Carter Sloane.

"I need a ride to your house, where we will both take showers and then we will talk."

"You want to use my shower?"

"Yes, now don't start asking the same questions over again. I don't think I can take it. Just lead me to your car, all right?"

"What if I don't want you to come home with me?"

He moved over to her and dropped on his haunches in front of her, then tilted her chin up with his fingertip. The touch was gentle, and his expression was more tender than she'd ever seen it. Not that she'd seen it all that often.

They didn't exactly move in the same circles.

"Then I'd have to convince you otherwise."

"This is really weird, Carter."

"Not from where I'm standing."

"You're nuts." Her hand flew to her mouth. He might have kissed her stupid and right into a mind-blowing orgasm, but he was still the man who owned the company she worked for.

"Not so much anymore."

"What does that mean?" Talking to him was like talking to a Chinese puzzle. Nothing made sense to her.

"Nothing important." He laid his hand on her knee. "Will you take me home with you so we can talk?"

"About marriage?" She had to ask. It was too incredible a concept for her to accept with equanimity.

"About a proposition I have for you that includes marriage."

Which cleared up a whole lot less than it muddled in her brain.

Chapter Three

Carter and Daisy both stopped beside the driver's side door of her yellow Xterra. He put his hand out for the keys.

She stared at it like it was a snake threatening to bite her. "What?"

"The keys." He was feeling pretty uncomfortable at the moment, and he wanted to get to her house and the shower.

He was also hoping that after they discussed his proposition and she agreed to it he could convince her to let him kiss her again . . . and a whole lot more.

The sooner they got to her house, the sooner he'd have his lips on hers again.

She shook her head. "Nobody drives my Xterra but me."

"You'll have to make an exception to the rule because I don't let anyone else drive me. Period."

"No." She pressed the unlock button.

He heard a snick as the lock buttons popped up.

"Look, Daisy, I'm serious about this."

Two small fists landed on hips just meant for a man's hands to cradle, and her expression turned downright mean. "So am I. If you want a ride, get in the car. Otherwise you can catch a taxi."

She didn't mean that.

She tapped her foot and looked meaningfully down at his trousers. He followed her gaze and ground his teeth. No way in Hades was he calling a taxi in this condition.

"I don't like other people driving me," he bit out, trying again to get through to her stubborn little brain.

"I'll make you like it."

"This isn't a joke."

She got all vulnerable and wounded looking, and he wanted to punch something. How did women do that?

"And kissing me was?"

"No, of course not. Did it feel like a joke when you were screaming like a banshee in my ear?"

She averted her face, embarrassed . . . again. He wondered how long that attitude would last once he got her in his bed on a regular basis.

"You told me you'd make me like your tongue, and I believed you."

"No, you didn't. You made me promise to stop if you hit my shoulder."

She shrugged, her sweet curves bouncing a little and scattering most of his concentration and pretty much all of his annoyance. "I still let you kiss me."

"That was more than a kiss." It was important to him that she acknowledge what had happened was bigger than that.

"Yes, it was."

"So, let's go to your house so we can talk and explore where some more kissing might lead us." And get him out of his clothes. Yeah, getting naked sounded really good.

She turned her head. "I drive."

He rolled his eyes. "N—"

"I told you I'd make you like it." She winked, and he lost it.

What was left of his righteous man-in-control-being-thwarted-by-a-sexy-little-termagant anger melted right out of him, and he laughed out loud. "Promise?"

She grinned, looking so cute he had to lean down and kiss her. Just once. Full on the lips.

He stepped back, and she gave him a dazed smile. "I promise."

He got in the passenger seat for the first time since he was eighteen.

Daisy lived in a renovated Victorian-era farmhouse on the outskirts of New Hope. The bright white exterior with wine trim and neatly manicured lawn fit her personality. Organized. Shy. Always well-groomed. It had been a toss-up for personnel whether to get her on the accounting track or marketing. Marketing had won by a very small margin.

She had creativity, but it was mixed with the mind of a bean counter, perfect for the marketing department.

She smiled as she parked her Xterra in the attached garage. "Did I make you like it?"

He took his white-knuckled grip off the dashboard and tried to think of something to say that wouldn't hurt her feelings. "You don't drive like I expected you to."

Sedate and carefully, like the woman who had edged her lawn with perfect precision should do.

One dark, shapely eyebrow cocked over her twinkling eye. "What does that mean?"

"Heck, Daisy, you drive like Mario Andretti on speed."

Far from looking hurt, she giggled. "I know. It's my only vice."

She pressed the button to lower the garage door and then got out of the car.

He followed her, his adrenaline pumping every bit as hard as it had been on the desk in her office. "It's a dangerous vice. I don't want you speeding anymore."

"I didn't open it up until we were on the highway."

"It doesn't matter. Driving like that is going to get you killed."

She stopped at the door to the outside and turned to face him, crossing her arms over her chest just like she had in her office. "How I drive is none of your business."

"It will be." And he'd make darn sure she did it safely or got chauffeured everywhere from here on out.

Her chin went so high in the air, he didn't know how she could see where she was going as she turned back around. "That remains to be seen."

Her hips swayed just enough to make him twitch with renewed sexual interest as they walked through the garage into the house.

Arguing with her turned him on. Big-time. Being with her at all did it, too. Heck, if he were honest with himself, and he usually was, he had to admit it took only thinking about her to get a hard-on that could double as a flagpole.

She led him to a guest bathroom. One entire wall had been painted to look like a plate glass window with a view of an old-fashioned rose garden. It looked so real, he could practically smell the flowers, and then he realized she had a bowl of dried rose petals on the back of the toilet.

The other walls were a soft wine color, and the countertop of burgundy tile shone as if she'd just polished it. From what he'd seen of the rest of her house on the way through, it was all done with the same eye for color and artistic appeal. No way could she afford an interior designer on her salary.

His eyes wandered back to the mural on the wall. "It's beautiful. Who painted it?"

"I did."

He spun to face her. "You did? It's amazing." And it explained how beautifully put together her house was.

Her chocolate brown eyes warmed with pleasure. "Thanks."

"I think you might be wasted in my marketing department."

She shook her head vehemently. "This kind of stuff is fun as a hobby. If you made it my job, I'd get bored with it. Besides, I like working for Sloane Electronics."

They were going to have to talk about that.

She might find it uncomfortable to keep her current position when she became his wife.

Taking a lot for granted, aren't you, buddy?

Not nearly as much as he wanted to.

"The towel on the shower rack is fresh."

Of course it was. "Thanks."

"I'll just let you take your shower, then."

He nodded, wondering if said towel would provide adequate covering for their discussion later. No way was he getting back into his pants.

They were write-offs, and he doubted she had anything that would fit him.

He stepped under the hot, pulsing spray, wishing Daisy had opted to join him. It would have been a whole lot more fun. The warm water restored some of his equilibrium, but he grimaced when he had to wash his hair with shampoo that smelled like the herbal tea a former secretary had drunk every morning at her desk. Chamomile, or something.

When he got out of the shower, a pair of running shorts and T-shirt were waiting on the vanity counter.

He hadn't heard her come in, which was probably a good thing since he might have done something he'd regret. Like drag her fully clothed into the shower with him.

He eyed the frosted glass door of the enclosure and wondered how much she'd seen when she'd brought the clothes in. Imagining her looking at his naked body did bad things to his self-control, and he forced his mind down different paths.

He slipped on the shorts and then the T-shirt. They fit way too well to be anything belonging to her. He wondered if he was wearing her dead husband's clothes. The thought gave him the creeps.

When he stepped out of the bathroom, he could hear a shower running somewhere else in the house. What would she do if he joined her? Would she get mad? Would she scream? Throw soap at him? Or . . . welcome him? She'd told him no to sharing a shower, so he had no way of finding out.

He wanted her to trust him, to know that when he gave his word, he kept it.

So, he went in search of the kitchen. He made pretty good coffee for a guy who'd had a housekeeper most of his life. He'd given up a lot of things when he went to New York to run the Sloane Electronics offices there.

He'd wanted to be independent, and that meant learning to do everything for himself, including the cooking.

The coffee was just finishing when she walked into the kitchen. She'd pulled her black hair up into a ponytail and changed from her work attire into a pair of navy blue flannel pajama bottoms with little white sheep all over them and a clingy T-shirt the same color as her pants. She looked cute and sexy. Very sexy.

Was she wearing a bra? He couldn't see the lines of one, and the longer he stared, the more pronounced her nipples got. Definitely no bra.

"Stop that!"

He looked up into snapping brown eyes. "Sorry."

She was blushing, which was something he realized he liked. It made him feel all man to evoke such a vulnerable reaction in her, plus it let him know her thoughts were running parallel to his own.

"Yes, well . . . is that coffee I smell?"

He gave her a look that told her he wasn't fooled by her bland conversation. He knew what she was thinking, and it was making him hard all over again. "Yeah."

"May I have some?"

He shrugged. "It's your house."

She nodded and scooted around him to get mugs down from the cupboard and fill them both with the fresh brew. "Do you want anything in yours?"

"No."

She handed him his mug, and he sat down, watching with amusement as she doctored her coffee with enough milk and sugar to turn it a soft shade of tan.

He shook his head as she sat down. "Why don't you just heat the milk up and add sugar to it?"

"I do, at night before bed sometimes." She sighed. "I probably shouldn't. I could stand to forgo the sugar on a lot of things, I guess."

"Why?"

She looked at him as though he was teasing her. "Come on, isn't it obvious? I need to lose a few pounds."

"You're kidding, right?" She wasn't anemic, but she wasn't too big either. "You're perfect."

"That's not what my husband thought."

He didn't have a good feeling about this. "What did he think?"

"That I was fat."

"He said that?" Good thing the guy was dead or Carter would have decked him.

"Yes. The women in his crowd thought anything bigger than a size three was moo-queen material."

"What were they, a bunch of drug addicts?"

He'd seen enough of that in New York. Pencil-thin women who kept their figures using recreational drugs. So, they were skinny as hell, but about as rational as a woman going through PMS.

She shocked him when she nodded. "Yes."

"What about your husband?"

"He died of an overdose of heroin."

He said a word his mother had told him never to use in front of a lady.

Daisy winced. "Yeah."

"I'm sorry."

"It's over."

"You're probably a little leery about marriage then, huh?" He hadn't expected that complication.

But she shrugged. "I don't know."

"Hey, I'm not wearing his clothes, am I?"

She smiled, shaking her head. "They're my brother's. He stays here when he's in town visiting the family."

"Where is he the rest of the time?"

"All over the world."

"What does he do?"

"He's a merc."

If she'd been going for shock value, she'd gotten it. In spades. *"Your brother is a mercenary?"*

"Amazing, isn't it, that a boring, plain Jane like me could have a brother who does something so scandalous? My little sister is a model, too, or at least she was until last year. I'm the unexciting one in the family."

"You don't bore me, or didn't you get that earlier?" How could she think so little of herself? "You're sexy."

She laughed, just as if he'd made a joke.

"I'm not kidding. Do you seriously think I come in my shorts for every woman I kiss?"

Her laughter dried up like a drop of water on an Arizona highway. She put her hands to pink cheeks. "Don't say things like that."

"All right, as long as you don't mind me doing them, because that's not an option."

She took a sip of her coffee, choked and started coughing to beat the band. He jumped up and got her a glass of water, made her drink at least half of it before sitting back down again.

"Tell me about your proposition," she said, still sounding a little wheezy.

"I want you to marry me. In exchange I'll settle a lump sum of five hundred thousand dollars on you."

Her coffee cup went flying, and they spent the next five minutes cleaning up the mess.

Afterward, he dragged her into the living room. "I think we better finish our discussion in here. The kitchen isn't a safe place for you."

She let him draw her down onto the couch. "It's not the kitchen. It's you. You just offered me a half a million dollars to marry you."

He didn't figure the problem was that she wanted more money. "My dad died four years ago."

"I know." She laid her hand on his thigh in comfort, but comforting feelings were not the ones heating up his insides at that small touch. "I'm sorry"

"Thanks. He left a will."

Her lips quirked. "Most men in his position would have."

"Not like this one."

"What do you mean?"

"The will stipulates that I have to be married within five years of his death or Sloane Electronics goes on the auction block and the proceeds are to be put in a memorial fund at the hospital in my father's name."

"That's ridiculous!"

"I agree. Unfortunately, it's also legit. My dad could not control the finances while he was alive, but he could control them in his death. My grandfather's will was a little screwy, too."

"I hope you aren't going to be so stupid."

"To try to control people with money?" He shook his

head. "No. Even the thought disgusts me." That's why he wanted to give her the lump sum on their marriage.

He didn't want her to feel trapped like his father had in a marriage he no longer wanted.

Not that Carter thought his dad's choices had been all that great, but too many people had been hurt by his mother's and his grandfather's use of money to control. Carter would never be guilty of that.

"So you want me to marry you in order for you to keep your company?"

"Yes. It's not my mother's only source of income, but it's a big part of it, and I've just worked out terms to split the company with my brothers." They'd both refused an equal split, but had agreed to take a small percentage of Sloane Electronics as part of their individual holdings. His brothers were every bit as determined as he was. "I'm not letting it go on the auction block."

"Brothers? I thought, I mean . . ."

"That Rand was my only brother?"

"Yes."

"Apparently my father didn't keep it zipped when he was out of town on business either . . . at least on one occasion. I've got a brother who's a year younger than me. We just found out about him not too long ago."

"What's he like?" She seemed totally diverted from the original subject.

"He looks like a football player with a crew cut, but he's about as conservative as any man I've ever met. I like him. So do Rand and Phoebe."

"You and Rand used to be enemies."

"I was never his enemy, not really, but it took our father dying and time away, living on my own, for me to accept I was his brother."

"And Rand accepted you, too?" she asked, sounding fascinated.

He wished it had been that easy. "That took some doing. He had a lot of reasons not to trust anyone named Sloane."

"But you're not like your father."

"Yeah, I finally figured that out, and so did he."

"What about your other brother?"

"Colton?"

"Is that his name?"

"Yes."

"Was he glad when you found him?"

"You know, he was. Of course, he knew about us, or me at least in a conceptual way, so he wasn't shocked when I called. His mom raised him pretty unconventionally, but he values family."

"That's really neat."

Four years ago, discovering he had another brother wouldn't have made him all that happy. He'd spent his childhood paying for his father's indiscretions, but he'd finally come to accept that good could come from bad, and he agreed with Daisy. Having a couple of brothers was in fact pretty neat. "Yeah."

"And you want to split your company with them?"

"It's not just my company. It's their heritage, too."

She didn't argue about it with him like his mother had, like his darned brothers had. She simply nodded. "Why don't you just contest the will?"

"That would bring a lot of media exposure, something that would hurt my mother." Appearances were all that mattered to Cassandra Sloane.

Again, that was not how he chose to live his life, but he loved his mother. As cold as she was, she was still the woman who had given him birth, and he owed her whatever protection he could give her from harm.

Besides, he liked the idea of marriage to Daisy.

She chewed on her bottom lip. "You're right, Mrs. Sloane wouldn't like that, but I don't think she'd like you marrying one of your employees either."

She'd have to come to terms with it. He'd made one mistake trying to marry a woman his mother would deem worthy. He wasn't about to make another.

"Unless you aren't planning to tell her?"

"What do you mean not tell her?" He turned toward Daisy, his knee coming up on the couch and brushing her thigh. "Of course I'll tell her. She's my mother."

"Oh." Her hands twisted in a knot in her lap. "I thought maybe you planned to keep it a secret and then get an annulment or something after the terms of the will were satisfied."

"Right. After today, do you really believe we can share a platonic marriage?" That was one of his chief reasons for wanting to marry her. He wanted her in his bed every night and as many mornings and afternoons as he could manage.

"But . . ."

"I want you in my bed, Daisy. All of the time."

"So, what you're really saying is that you want to pay me to go to bed with you and fulfill the terms of your father's will?"

Chapter Four

Daisy watched in fascinated wonder as Carter seemed to swell with indignation. His chest puffed. His eyes narrowed. His expression went completely rigid.

"I don't need to pay a woman to go to bed with me."

"So you *don't* want me to go to bed with you?"

"That's not what I said."

She smiled. That's what she thought, but it paid to be sure. "So, you do want me?"

"Yes."

"And you want to pay me?"

He jumped up and stared down at her, wrath glittering in his blue eyes, making them look much darker than usual. "I'm not paying you to have sex with me."

"You're paying me to marry you."

He relaxed a little. "Yes."

"And you don't want the marriage to be platonic. I mean, you're planning on consummating it and everything."

"I plan to do a whole lot more than just consummate our marriage."

She actually shivered from the sensual promise in his voice.

"And you want to pay me five hundred thousand dollars to do it." It was a lot of money.

"I want you to have options," he bit out from between clenched teeth, "to be able to end the marriage whenever you want to."

"So, this marriage doesn't have a time limit?" She wondered why not. He couldn't really want to be stuck with her for the rest of his life.

"Our marriage will be as permanent as any other marriage."

That could be taken a lot of ways.

"You mean you want kids and everything?" This was getting stranger by the minute.

He shrugged. "Yeah. I guess. If we think that's a good idea sometime in the future."

"You don't love me."

His face went stiff. "I'm not good at love, but I know I can do fidelity. Boy, do I know."

She wondered at the frustration in his voice, but she didn't ask about it. She was more interested in his assertion he wasn't good at love. "You loved Phoebe."

"I wanted to marry Phoebe and I cared about her, but I don't think I'm any more capable of real love than my father was."

From all that she'd heard about Hoyt Sloane, that was pretty self-denigrating, not to mention unbelievable in her estimation. "I don't think you're like your father."

"In some ways I'm not." Again that enigmatic frustration laced his voice.

"What if you fall in love with someone else?"

"Not going to happen." He sounded very sure of that. Too sure.

"Are you still in love with Phoebe? Did you come back expecting to marry her and find out she'd fallen for your brother?" Scenarios were spinning through her head more quickly than a movie reel on fast forward.

"I am not still in love with Phoebe."

"But did you come back planning to marry her?" she pressed.

When Carter wanted to hide his feelings, he did it very well. Absolutely no emotion showed on his face. "I want to marry you *now*, and that's all that matters."

"And you want to pay me." She couldn't quite get over that aspect to the situation. "A lot of money."

"Yes."

"And you want me to go to bed with you. Every night."

Blue fire scorched her from his eyes. "Yes."

"So, *you are paying me to go to bed with you.*" What else could it be? He didn't know her well enough to care about her in any other sense. "I guess the kiss in the office was a test trial of sorts, wasn't it?"

An expression of discomfort overcame his features. "You could call it that."

"I must have passed." Amazing, really, when she considered how often she'd failed that particular test in the past.

"I'm now certain the passion is explosive and mutual if that's what you mean."

"But how can you be sure I'll be a good wife? I could be a closet kleptomaniac or something."

"I had you checked out." He said it so casually, as if that was what all men planning to get married did.

"That's despicable."

"It's smart."

"How would you feel if I had you investigated?" she demanded, even while acknowledging to herself that if she'd been smart enough to have her future husband investigated when she was twenty, she would never have gotten married.

"What would be the point?" He rolled his shoulders back, molding the muscles of his chest with the tight cotton of his shirt.

128 / Lucy Monroe

Her eyes traveled down to shorts that hinted at even more delightful wonders below. It was all she could do not to drool.

Apparently oblivious to her lascivious thoughts, he dropped back onto the sofa beside her. "My whole life has been on display and the subject of New Hope gossip since the day I was born. Paying to have me investigated would be overkill."

He didn't sound bitter, just resigned. And he was right. She did know a lot about him. More than she wanted to. Enough to fall in love with a man who although he wasn't a fantasy, might as well have been. He'd been just as unreachable.

Totally unattainable and yet she had been unable to stop thinking about him since the first time she'd seen him. He'd been visiting her department, the wiz-kid, heir apparent. Not to mention gorgeous and totally sexy.

She'd cried the day she read the announcement of his engagement to Phoebe. And told herself she was an idiot for doing so.

It all started when she learned what kind of childhood he'd had. A father who was a philanderer and a mother who made ice seem warm by comparison were so different from her own affection-filled household growing up. The knowledge had kindled feelings that had grown over the years into something as intimate as they were inappropriate and hopeless.

Only now the fantasy was coming true, and, *"You're paying me a half a million dollars to have sex with you."*

For a woman voted by her first husband as least likely to entice a man into bed, the idea of being paid for such an arrangement had a strange, heady appeal.

Carter looked ready to explode, though.

She ignored the blustering. He didn't love her, but she could gain a lot of satisfaction from knowing he wanted her, Daisy Jackson, enough to not only marry her, but to pay her lots and lots of money to go to bed with him.

Okay, he needed a wife to fulfill the terms of his father's will, too, but he could have married someone else, someone from his social set. He'd chosen her.

His father had been a womanizer of the first order, but his brother was the faithful kind, or at least he had been in his first marriage and showed no inclination to flirt with other women now that he was married to Phoebe. It had always been Daisy's opinion that Carter was a lot more like Rand than he was like Hoyt Sloane.

The clincher, though, was the certainty that if she said no, he'd find some other woman. He had to get married. That was a fact, and she wasn't so simpleminded she thought he'd hang around moping if she turned him down.

His engagement to Phoebe had hurt her; watching him marry another woman after he'd offered her the opportunity to be the one would kill her.

"Okay."

He'd been going on again about how he didn't need to pay women for sex, had never bought a prostitute in his whole life, yadda, yadda, yadda, but at her one word, he went silent as the inside of an airtight drum.

Carter couldn't believe she'd agreed.

He'd been sure she was too offended by the idea he was paying her for sex to go through with it. Apparently he'd been wrong. Far from angry, she looked very pleased with herself.

"You're going to marry me?"

"Yes."

"You understand that though I need to get married to fulfill the terms of my father's will, I consider this every bit as binding as any other marriage?" He needed to make sure she got that aspect of the situation.

He had no desire to marry her and then divorce her six months down the road. He'd spent four years wanting her and figured it would take at least that long to wear a slight edge off of his desire for her. He wasn't sure he could ever satisfy it.

"We're not marrying for love, but we're marrying for life, right?"

He nodded, relieved she didn't seem to mind about the love thing.

"And if I love you . . . is that going to bother you?"

The question stumped him. How did he feel about her falling in love with him?

Her head cocked to one side. "Is it that difficult of a question?"

"No."

"So?"

He thought of the way Phoebe looked at Rand, the sense of peace his brother seemed to have when he was around her. "You can fall in love with me if you want."

"Thank you." She said it politely, but her lips twitched.

He grimaced. "That sounded pretty arrogant, I guess."

She shrugged, and his gaze locked in on the movement of her generous curves. He could slip his hand inside her T-shirt and touch her with no problem at all.

"If this marriage is forever . . ."

Forever. That sounded good. "Yeah?"

"I want children, as in plural." She bit her lip and looked at him appealingly. "Not right away, but I definitely want them. Once we're sure the marriage is going to work."

Any man who saw that look and wasn't moved by it would have to be stone dead in the region of his heart. "Okay. I would have liked brothers and sisters—*that actually lived with me growing up,*" he clarified.

Her chocolate brown gaze melted with an understanding that made him uncomfortable.

"Hey, it's no big deal. I've got two brothers now."

She nodded. "I'd like to meet them. I mean, I've seen Rand a few times and even met him at a charity-a-thon I was running in. He's gorgeous, but I've never even seen your other brother."

He did not like hearing her call Rand gorgeous. "You're not marrying my brothers."

She laughed. "I wouldn't want to."

"But you do want to marry me?"

"Yes."

"And you don't have a problem with it being a real marriage?"

"I wouldn't consider any other kind."

So, the passion was important to her, too. Good.

He moved closer to her, inhaling her scent and letting loose the desire inside him he'd kept leashed to have this conversation.

Her soft brown eyes widened. "Carter?"

"I think we should celebrate our engagement."

She leaned back until the couch stopped her from going any farther.

He followed her, stopping when his lips hovered just above hers, and he put his hands on either side of her head. "Don't you?"

"C-celebrate?"

To answer, he put his mouth over hers. She tasted faintly of coffee, but her own sweet flavor overrode anything else. Her mouth was everything and more he had dreamed it would be. Soft. Tantalizing. Luscious.

He played at the seam of her lips with his tongue until she opened her mouth on a small sigh. Her hands tunneled under his T-shirt, and the feel of those sweet little fingers on his stomach sent his already erect flesh into a state of raging excitement.

He wanted her.

Now.

He grabbed the hem of her shirt and pulled it off. She let him, but made a small noise of unhappiness when she had to stop touching him to get the shirt off. As soon as it was out of the way, she went back to touching him.

Now that she was naked, at least on top, he wanted to be, too—so he could feel her chest against his, something he had not been able to do during the nuclear meltdown kiss they'd shared in her office.

Fabric ripped as he yanked the shirt off.

She giggled, but her laughter stopped when he pressed his hot skin against hers.

Turgid points pressed into his pecs while the softness of her breasts molded him. Man, it felt good. Too good. The urge to be inside her grew to gigantic proportions, but he wasn't going to hurry. No way. There was too much he wanted to see and do first.

He pulled back so he could look at her. Her breasts were flawless. Round. Firm. The perfect size to fill his big hands. Tip-tilted, hard nipples the color of ripe raspberries just begged to be suckled and laved with his tongue. The creamy fullness tempted him to touch and tease.

"You're beautiful."

"So are you."

He looked up at the sound of such husky words coming from her.

Her eyelids were at half-mast, not quite hiding the expression of want burning in their chocolate depths.

"Men are not beautiful."

"Whoever said that has never seen you."

Oh, man. He was going to lose it. With a growl he couldn't begin to suppress, he landed on top of her and started kissing her again.

She kissed him back, her need every bit as ferocious as his own.

Her hips arched up toward him, and he pressed into her.

It was wild.

It was hot.

He was going to come in his shorts again if he didn't do something fast.

He broke his mouth away from hers. "Where's the bedroom?"

"What's wrong with the couch?"

"Not a damn thing, but we need protection."

She went completely still beneath him. "You mean a condom?"

"Yeah." Hell, he'd settle for her telling him she was on the pill right now. No way was she a health risk. She wasn't promiscuous, and he knew he was clean. "Are you on the pill, honey?"

"No."

"Okay, then we need a condom." He would definitely prefer to go without one. He wanted to be closer to her than he'd ever been to another woman physically, but they'd both agreed that children were a future undertaking.

"I don't have one."

He reared up like someone had hit his ass with a cattle prod. "What?"

"I don't have condoms."

"Why not?" Didn't she care about safe sex?

"Because I don't need them."

"That's not a safe attitude to take, Daisy."

"It is for me."

His Daisy wasn't dumb enough to think she was immune to STDs, so there had to be another reason. "Why?"

She crossed her arms over her gorgeous breasts, and he wanted to howl at them being covered up. "Because I'm not sexually active."

"Not sexually active?" he parroted, not taking in what she was saying very well.

It was hard to think with her half-naked in front of him.

"As in I am not currently engaged in a sexual relationship, nor have I been for a long time."

"*How* long are we talking here?"

She glared, and her lips sealed like zip-lock.

"Come on. You can tell me."

"Six years," she burst out, sounding both embarrassed and angry she'd had to admit it. "I haven't had sex since my husband died."

Chapter Five

"Why the hell not?"

Okay, he'd had his own experience with celibacy, but it had not lasted *six* years. How had she stood it?

"I'm not a very sexual person."

He laughed out loud, but she didn't even crack a smile. She meant it.

"Right." He rocked his hard penis against her mound, and she moaned, her eyes going glazed with renewed passion, just that fast. "Tell me again how not sexual you are."

"I'm not," she said on a sigh and tipped up toward him. "At least not with anyone else. You bring out stuff in me I didn't know I could feel."

As much as he loved hearing that, he was ready to explode, and he didn't have a condom either. How stupid could he get? He'd known what he wanted when he came here. "I don't have anything either."

Her eyes widened, then filled with tears, and she hit his shoulder.

"Ouch! What was that for?"

"You started this, and now you tell me we can't finish it?"

"I'll take your car and go buy some, all right?" He'd offer

to do something else, anything else . . . but the truth was he wanted it all. He needed to come sheathed inside her.

Her head turned away from him, and then she went rigid. "Oh, no!"

"What?" He looked around, half expecting to see someone standing in the living room entrance, but it was empty.

"It's almost eight o'clock!"

"So? You're usually working this late. Don't tell me you have a hot date." Though, looking down at her, passion stamped on her like a brand, he didn't think it was such a far-off possibility.

She looked sexy enough to have six guys lined up on a string.

"You could say that."

His heart slammed into his chest. No way was he letting her go out with someone else. "Call and cancel."

"Are you jealous?" She looked at him as though he was a strange new species of insect, all curiosity and wide eyes.

"We're engaged. You can't go out with another man, and while we're on the subject, I don't believe in open marriages."

Her expression turned to one of outrage. "I don't either. What an awful thing to suggest!"

"Then no date."

She smirked. "I can't cancel this one."

"Like hell—"

"It's to babysit my sister's little girl."

"Your sister has a baby?"

"Yes. She's got a husband, too, and they're up here from Texas, visiting my parents. Tonight, they're all going to attend the local symphony."

"And you're supposed to watch the kid."

"Right. They should be here any minute."

The doorbell rang.

He could not believe his luck. "It looks like they just arrived."

She wasn't listening. She was too busy trying to shove
off of her. He helped her out by getting up.

"Thanks." She grabbed for her T-shirt and yanked i
over her head. Inside out.

He tugged on the tag attached to the collar. "I think th
supposed to go on the inside."

She frowned. "Shoot!" She was taking it off and revers
it as she crossed the living room.

The doorbell pealed again. Carter grabbed his borrow
T-shirt, saw it was a dead loss and figured her brother h
probably left more than one shirt behind. He went lookin
He found the guest room in the first room he tried. He'd lik
to see where she slept, but that would have to wait.

Sure enough, there were some more clothes in the top drawe
of a tallboy dresser standing against one wall. He found a plain
white T-shirt and pulled it on. It fit a little more loosely than
the first one.

Daisy breathed a sigh of relief that Carter had decided to
make himself scarce and save her awkward explanations
with her sister and brother-in-law. Not that explaining a run-
away marriage was going to be easy, but that was later, not
now, when she was still reeling from shock and unfulfilled
sexual desire.

Bella handed Daisy the diaper bag while her husband laid
the baby in the portable crib they'd brought along. "She should
sleep the whole time we're gone, but if she doesn't, there are
two bottles in the diaper bag." She pulled two short, plastic
baby bottles out of one of the cavernous side pockets to the
bag. "They should probably go in the fridge."

"I'll take those."

Daisy and Bella both spun toward the doorway at the
sound of Carter's voice. He'd pitched it low, evidently having
heard that her niece was sleeping.

He'd found another shirt, was her first thought on the sight of him. *Oh, crap*, was her second.

Sure enough, Bella's mouth formed in a surprised O while Jake came over from tucking his baby girl in to size Carter up.

He put his hand out, "Jake Barton."

Carter shook the other man's hand. "Carter Sloane."

"*The* Carter Sloane?" Bella asked, her shock obvious.

"I only know one Carter Sloane," Daisy answered before Carter could open his mouth.

"What's your boss doing here?"

"Technically, even though he owns the company I work for, he's not my boss."

Bella gave her that I-can't-believe-you'd-worry-about-a-little-thing-like-that look. "Regardless, what is he doing here? You said you were taking the night off."

"I am."

"My being here has nothing to do with Sloane Electronics," Carter smoothly inserted.

That wasn't strictly true either, but this time Daisy kept her mouth shut.

Bella eyed Carter's clothes with avid interest. "Is this like a date, or something?"

Little sisters could be the very devil. Daisy glared at her willowy sister to absolutely no effect.

Bella was too busy eyeing Carter.

He slid his arm around Daisy's shoulders. "Or something. We're engaged."

Nerves exploded inside her like a bomb detonated by Carter's admission. She was in for it now.

Bella staggered back a step. "But we didn't even know she was dating you." She turned to her husband. "Did we?"

"No." Jake wore his usual taciturn expression.

It changed only when he looked at his wife. Daisy would give a lot to have that kind of impact on Carter.

Carter kissed the top of Daisy's head. "It's all been pretty sudden."

"It must have been. She doesn't even have a ring." Bella sounded scandalized by the fact, and it was all Daisy could do not to laugh.

Trust her little sister to worry about something like that in the face of such a shocking revelation.

"She does. I hadn't given it to her yet because my proposal didn't exactly go as I'd planned."

It was Daisy's turn to be stunned. Her head snapped around to look at him. "I have a ring?"

He smiled indulgently at her, just like a real fiancée. "Oh, yeah."

He dropped his arm from around her shoulders to take her hand in his and then slid the most gorgeous diamond ring she'd ever seen on her third finger.

"It's . . ." She swallowed, inexplicably unable to speak.

"Gorgeous." Bella managed to infuse her whisper with the sense she had shouted the word. "Wow. You've got good taste in jewelry as well as women, Mr. Sloane."

"Carter. We're going to be related before long." The epitome of confident charm, he smiled at Bella.

Daisy didn't know about her sister, but her own insides were turning to mush from all that male charisma.

"It's going to be hard not to tell Mom and Dad when we see them at the theater."

Jake stepped forward and took his wife's arm. "Speaking of, we'd best be on our way, sweetheart."

Bella groaned. "I'd rather stay and hear details."

"Later."

Bella and Jake left, her sister giving last minute instructions on care for the baby interspersed with exclamations about Daisy's forthcoming marriage right up until Jake started the car engine.

Daisy walked back into the house with Carter's arm once

again around her. She led him into the kitchen where they stored the baby bottles in the fridge. "Are you hungry? We haven't had dinner."

"Are you offering to cook?"

"I made a Crock-Pot of beef stew yesterday. I can zap some in the microwave and make some toast to go with it. Biscuits would take too long to be worth it this late, I think."

"I'll make the toast. You heat the stew."

She watched in surprise as he went in search of bread. Before long he had four pieces of toast going, and she had to remind herself to get a move on with the stew.

"I can't believe you told my sister."

"Were you going to try to keep it a secret?"

"No, of course not. I just thought it would be easier to explain a quicky Vegas wedding after the fact, rather than before. Mom is going to kick up a fuss about not being there."

"Who said anything about Vegas?"

She closed the microwave door on a bowl with enough stew to feed her and Carter and turned the appliance on before turning to face him. He leaned against the counter with an air of relaxation she was far from feeling.

"I didn't mean Vegas literally. It's just that we're not going to have a regular wedding."

"Why not?"

Was he serious?

"For one, I don't want one. I have no desire to be the center of attention with a bunch of rich people trying to mingle with my friends and family. I still remember Bella's wedding, and it was awful."

"Jake's friends overwhelmed you, I take it?"

She nodded, feeling stupid. "I don't like big gatherings like that. Is that going to be a problem for you?"

Carter hadn't done a lot of socializing since coming back from New York, but maybe he wanted to.

"No. I don't like big groups either. Sometimes a man in my position can't avoid them, but I have no problem with having a small wedding. Just my family and yours."

"*You want your mother there?*"

The toaster popped open, and Carter turned away to butter the bread. "Sure. Don't you want your family there?"

"I guess, but that would mean Bella coming back for it."

"Or we could get married before she leaves."

"But that's next week." Shock upon shock coursed through her, and he stood there slicing toast as if they were discussing the weather.

"We can file for the marriage license tomorrow and pick it up on Monday. We can get married Tuesday."

"You want to get married in four days?"

He laid the toast on two small plates she'd pulled from the cupboard. "I'd rather get married tonight, but I can wait four days."

They weren't exactly marrying for normal reasons, even if he did want the marriage to be a regular one. There was no reason for a long engagement, and for all she knew the will had some sort of stipulation on how long he had to be married before the five year anniversary.

When she asked about it, Carter shook his head. "No. Nothing like that, but, Daisy, I want you, and four days is going to feel like four years as it is."

"But you don't have to wait. We could buy condoms tonight, and after my sister picks up the baby . . ." She let her voice trail off when he shook his head.

"You've gone without sex for six years. That's got to mean something."

"I told you. I didn't really mind about that." She'd wanted only one man in six years, but he'd been completely out of her league. Carter Sloane. Now she got to have him, and she didn't want to wait four hours, much less four days.

"Daisy, did you have sex before you were married?"

Heat scorched into her cheeks. "What difference does that make?"

"Honey, I'm going to be your husband. You can tell me intimate stuff like this without blushing."

Right. "You didn't answer me."

"It matters. Now tell me."

"No." The microwave dinged, and she pulled the stew out. "I didn't have a lover before I got married."

And what she'd had after marriage had been really dismal. If she and Carter hadn't shared such an amazingly passionate kiss in her office and later on her couch, she would be really worried about this marriage for the sake of sex and fulfilling a will thing.

"So, basically, you've made love with one man, and he was a dud, or you wouldn't have been so convinced you weren't all that sexual, right?"

She gritted her teeth and nodded. He didn't have to put it like that, truth or not.

"So, you deserve a wedding night to end all wedding nights, and I'm just the man to give it to you."

She would have accused him of gross arrogance if she hadn't been a second away from melting to the kitchen floor in a puddle from the sensual promise in his eyes.

The next three days were torture for Daisy. Carter insisted on taking her to meet his mother. Mrs. Sloane had been accepting of her son's marriage plans, but by no means warm toward her daughter-in-law to be. Since she knew about the will and the implications of Carter remaining unmarried, that made sense, but it had been very uncomfortable for Daisy.

If that wasn't bad enough, Daisy's own mother and her sister insisted on helping her pick out her wedding gown. They'd argued over the color until they found a tea-length gown in antique lace that fit her like a dream. Both women thought it was beautiful and gave it a thumbs-up. Daisy felt naked from the waist up wearing it.

At least she had more cleavage showing than with any other dress or shirt she owned. She'd even been forced to buy a new bra because of the low-cut bodice.

She'd agreed to it only because one more hour of shopping with two women who were intent on prizing the details of Daisy's supposed secret courtship with Carter out of her would have driven her stark staring bonkers

She refused to lie to her mother and sister and told them as much of the truth as she could.

She'd loved Carter for years, and when he started showing an interest in her, she'd gone under without taking an extra breath of air.

Bella understood because she'd married Jake very soon after meeting him.

Daisy's mother had been more skeptical, but she wanted her daughter's happiness, and a person would have to be blind not to realize Daisy was happy.

Carter seemed pretty pleased with the deal himself, and that added to Daisy's sense of joy.

He wanted to marry her.

He really did.

Even if it was just to get her into bed and keep her there, at least it was personal, and he wasn't looking to get something from her like her first husband. He wanted her.

He could have married anyone, and he'd chosen her. She couldn't quite figure out why yet, but his ardor was unquestionable. Why he wanted plain Daisy Jackson to the exclusion of all other women, she didn't know, but she didn't care either.

It was a reality she was more than happy to live with.

Daisy was organizing her closet to make room for Carter's things when the doorbell rang.

She jogged down the stairs to answer it. Carter waited on her front porch, a wolfish expression in his eyes that was beginning to make her nervous.

He'd worn that exact expression every single time they'd seen each other in the past three days, and that had been quite often. Not only had there been dinner with his mother, but he dropped into her office several times throughout the day. She would have thought he would be too busy, but he made the time to see her. He also insisted on eating every meal with her and would have gone shopping with them for the wedding dress if her mother hadn't thrown a hissy fit.

"You going to let me in?"

She stepped back. "Sure, but why are you here?"

Their wedding was the next day, and he'd said nothing about coming over tonight.

He came inside and shut the door. "I brought you a present."

"Oh, no . . . I don't want . . ." She didn't know what she wanted to say. They'd seen the lawyer earlier today, and Carter had transferred the five hundred thousand dollars into an account with an investment firm in her name.

They'd also signed pre-nups, and she was feeling sort of weird about all the money stuff.

"It's really a present for me." He took her arm. "Come on. You can open it in the living room."

He pulled her to sit beside him on the couch and then dropped a gift bag from Victoria's Secret in her lap.

She could feel the blush already starting, and she hadn't even removed the pink tissue yet.

"I want you to wear this under your wedding dress tomorrow. I want to think of it on you."

She stared at him. His eyes were the color of the sky at midnight, and they mesmerized her with their intensity.

"What is it?"

He leaned forward and kissed her. Just once, but with

enough impact to steal her breath. He'd done a lot of that in the past three days, but he never let it go beyond a casual kiss. No inferno kisses burning up their bodies with need.

"Open it and find out."

So she did, pulling the tissue out and dropping it on the floor. Then she pulled out a bra that made the one she'd bought to wear under her dress look like it should belong to her grandmother. This one was a demibra made of off-white satin with just enough boning and padding that she knew it would push her cleavage up to a whole new level.

"I don't wear push-up bras. I'm too big."

"Wear it, just this once for me."

She swallowed and made no promises. Then she pulled out a pair of panties that looked like a triangle of satin and some ribbon. "It's a thong."

Oh, my goodness. Nice women raised in New Hope did not go around wearing thongs.

He winked. "They're going to look great on you."

She bit her lip and pulled the remaining item out of the bag, wondering what it would be. It was a pair of stay-ups. Thigh-high stockings with rubberized lace to make them stay up.

She fingered the sheer, silky fabric.

"You want me to wear all this under my wedding dress?"

He brushed her hair back from her neck and rested his warm hand there. "And nothing else. Will you do that for me, honey?"

She lifted her gaze from the lingerie to his face. His features were rigid with an emotion that left her feeling breathless. "I've never worn stuff like that. I'll feel silly."

"No, you won't. You'll feel sexy knowing you're wearing it just for me and that I know, too. You'll get hot thinking about me trying to undress you in my mind."

"During my wedding ceremony?" She was doing that Minnie Mouse thing again.

He leaned forward and kissed her again, lingering in a

way he hadn't done in three days. "Yeah," he said against her lips.

Then he kissed her like he meant it, and she lost track of where she was, or anything else. When he stopped kissing her, she was in his lap with her hands buried deep in his hair and the press of his erection against her hip.

"So, are you going to do it?"

"Yes."

"Good." He kissed her on the tip of her nose. "I like it that you're so shy. You're practically a virgin."

"You can't be practically a virgin." And he didn't need to rub in how much more experience he had than her. "You are, or you aren't, and I'm not." Despite the fact it had been so long since she'd last made love.

No way would Carter ever have gone six years without sex. She doubted he could go more than a few weeks.

"Aw, honey, you're so cute when you get all offended and bristly."

"Did you want me to wear those scraps of silk, or not?"

He kissed her again in answer, and this time when they came up for air, she collapsed against him. "I want you."

"I want you, too, and tomorrow night I'll have you."

It sounded like a threat as much as a promise, and she shivered.

He smiled that wolf's smile again and stood up, setting her gently on the sofa. "I better leave now, or I won't leave at all."

"It was your idea to wait until tomorrow night," she reminded him.

"Yes, it was. You may not know the power of anticipation, little innocent, but I do."

"If you'd wanted a more experienced woman, I'm sure you could have gotten one and could have paid a whole lot less than half a million dollars for the privilege," she said, feeling stung by his teasing.

She was too sexually frustrated to find much of anything amusing at the moment.

It was his turn to look frustrated. "I'm not paying you to go to bed with me."

"Whatever." Which told him he could think what he liked, but she knew the truth.

"Watch it, sweetheart. I'm on a hair trigger, and I don't think you want to deal with the consequences if I go off."

She stood up, ignoring the lingerie scattered around her, and put her hands on her hips. "Are you sure about that?"

He laughed. "Wait until tomorrow night and find out."

"If you're so worried I can't handle you—" She didn't get the chance to finish.

He'd crossed the room in three long strides and put one arm around her and the other hand over her mouth. "You're going to handle me all right. Just the way I want. And for the record, I don't want a woman who is more experienced. I want you."

He moved his hand, but when she opened her mouth to answer, his was there. Hot lips devoured her own until she was clinging like ivy to his powerful build.

He pulled back and peeled her away from him. "Hold that thought. Hold it real tight."

Stupefied from desire, she just watched him walk away. She didn't move again until several minutes after she heard the front door close.

Boy, that man could kiss.

Carter went to meet his brothers at the Dark Herring after leaving Daisy's house. Colton had flown in that morning so he could be there for the wedding, and he and Rand said they wanted to celebrate Carter's upcoming marriage with him.

The other men were already sitting at a small table in the back when he got inside the bar. Colton had a coffee in front of him. Carter had been surprised to discover his younger brother didn't drink. At all. Rand, on the other hand, was sipping on whiskey. Carter ordered a screwdriver from the bar before sitting down to join them.

"You look mussed," Rand said, his mouth curved knowingly.

Carter finger-combed his hair, realizing he had done nothing to tame it after the incendiary kiss he'd shared with Daisy. "I went by to see my fiancée."

He liked the way that sounded, but he was going to like the word "wife" even better.

Colton didn't smile. The big man hardly ever did, from what Carter could see. His younger brother wasn't dour, not really. Sober probably described him best. Sober and conservative. He and Rand were almost total opposites, and yet, since meeting, they'd gotten along like . . . well, like long, lost brothers.

"So, you're not merely marrying the woman to fulfill Hoyt's stupid will?" Colton asked, sounding suspicious.

"Wanting her doesn't mean loving her," Rand pointed out.

Carter hadn't been expecting this, but maybe he should have. Neither of his brothers was the shy type, and he didn't think it would sit well with them if they thought he was getting married for their sakes or even for his mother's.

"I want to marry Daisy," he reassured them.

"Why now?" Rand asked.

"What do you mean *why now?*"

"You came home from New York after a four-year absence, and all of a sudden you're engaged to marry one of your employees, a woman you've never dated and haven't seen in four years. I have a hard time believing it doesn't have anything to do with Hoyt's will."

"And if it does?"

His older brother's eyes narrowed. "If that's the case, it's a stupid thing to do."

"Marrying Daisy is not stupid."

"It is if you're doing it just to keep Sloane Electronics. The will is so screwy, any good lawyer worth his retainer could break it."

"Not without a lot of media fanfare," Carter pointed out.

Colton shifted his linebacker-sized shoulders. "So, you *are* getting married because of it."

"It plays a part," Carter admitted, "in the timing anyway, but marrying Daisy isn't all about the will."

"Do you love her?" Colton asked, sounding curious, but not condemning.

"I want her. Obsessively." Would his brothers understand that kind of desire?

He'd never felt it before Daisy, and he doubted another woman existed in the world that he would react to with such strong libidinous tendencies.

Rand considered him, and Carter felt as if he was being probed for secrets. "Phoebe told me you left because you were sexually attracted to another woman. Was that Daisy?"

He saw no reason to deny it. "Yes."

"You've wanted her for four years?" Colton asked, having heard the story of Carter and Phoebe's aborted engagement from Phoebe the first time they met.

She said family shouldn't have secrets from each other.

Carter nodded. "And I'm going to have her."

"Is it true you're paying her to marry you?" Rand sounded just like anyone's older brother interrogating him about doing something he didn't agree with.

It was odd, but Carter found it didn't irritate him.

"How did you hear about that?"

"Your banker is also my banker."

And confidentiality was not what it was cracked up to be in a small town like New Hope. "He damn well better not have told anyone else."

Carter didn't want Daisy embarrassed.

"I told him that. I don't think it will be a problem. He doesn't want to lose the business of both Alexander Computers and Sloane Electronics."

"Thanks."

"So, what gives with the money?" Rand asked, proving he wasn't easily sidetracked.

"I don't want her feeling trapped in the marriage if she wants out later."

Both of his brothers nodded, and he knew they understood his reasoning.

"Is she marrying you for the money?" Colton asked.

"You're pretty damn blunt."

Colton almost smiled. "It's a family trait from what I can tell."

"The answer is that I don't know. I don't think so, but I have to tell you, at this point I also don't care." Which wasn't strictly true, but close enough. "If I don't make love to her soon, my balls are going to turn blue and fall off."

Both his brothers laughed. It was the first time he'd seen his younger brother do so, but Colton got serious again pretty fast. "Is she holding out for marriage?"

"No. I'm the one that's insisting on waiting for the wedding night."

"She's special, then." Rand sounded satisfied by the thought.

"Yes, she is." Daisy Jackson was very special, and soon she would be his.

He couldn't wait.

Chapter Six

Carter stood at the front of the small church, impatient for Daisy to walk down the aisle. Although the guest list was limited, he'd insisted on observing as many traditions as possible. He wanted Daisy to *feel* married, not like a woman who was being paid to go to bed with him.

Rand and Phoebe were there, making eyes at each other and smiling like idiots. Colton was his best man. That had been Rand's idea. Carter thought it was a good one. His mother sat in the front of the church, pretending none of the others were there. She'd deigned to speak with Daisy's parents earlier, but only to cover the most basic social niceties.

Appearances again.

He really didn't care. As long as she maintained a courteous demeanor with his wife and her family, his mother could continue to live in her frozen world of social pretense. But he'd made it clear to her that if she did anything to make Daisy unhappy, Carter would cut her right out of his life. He didn't think she'd miss him, but it would hurt her pride to have a public rift between them.

He had no doubt she'd play nice.

The organ music started, swelling to fill the small church. Daisy's sister came down the aisle first, smiling to beat the band. She was very happy for her older sibling and had told Carter as much.

He forgot all about Bella and her approval because Daisy was there. Framed in the entryway, she looked so sexy, his cock stood up and saluted. Her dress did an incredible job of outlining her curves, while appearing old-fashioned with its antique lace and full skirt. The neckline put enticing cleavage on display that would have made him drool if his mouth wasn't so dry. Her make-love-to-me-while-I'm-wearing-them spiked heels made her calves look long and enticing.

Oh, man, he was going to embarrass himself in front of the minister and their guests. He tried reciting stock prices in his head as she walked down the aisle toward him, but lost focus for anything but her when her pretty brown eyes met his.

She looked nervous and a little scared.

He didn't want her scared. Or nervous. Regardless of the reasons for it, this marriage was going to be good.

The passion was going to be fantastic.

He caught her gaze with his own and put his hand out to draw her to him. Someone made a choking noise that sounded like a stifled laugh, but he ignored it.

Daisy didn't seem to notice either. Ignoring the minister and his earlier advice for her to stop and face him when she reached the front of the church, she walked right up to Carter and put her hand in his.

It was so small, reminding him that it was his job to protect her. It was also cold.

He squeezed it. "It's going to be all right."

She smiled and laced her fingers with his, holding on tight. "I know."

Her voice only shook a little.

They turned to face the minister together.

* * *

Daisy's nerves got worse as the reception wore on. Carter was acting like a man who couldn't wait to get his bride to bed. Which she should have expected, but it overwhelmed her just the same. Right now, they were dancing so close she could feel his erection pressing against her belly. Physical evidence of what she was expected to deal with when they were alone.

Sex. Hot and consuming.

The closer the time came for them to leave, the more doubts she had about her ability to satisfy such blatant sexual urgency.

What if the passionate kisses they'd shared were a one-of thing? What if she was a dud when it came to actually having intercourse?

She might disappoint Carter like she had her first husband. Carter was so much more experienced than she was and probably used to a partner who knew what she was doing, knew how to make it good for him. Daisy was a sexual novice, and that wasn't the only place they differed.

Carter owned a multinational company, bought his suits from an exclusive tailor in London and had grown up rubbing elbows with the rich and famous. She'd been in the workforce since graduating from high school, wore clothes she'd found on sale at local department stores and got a rash merely thinking about meeting someone famous.

Daisy couldn't get rid of the feeling Carter had come back to New Hope with the intention of renewing a relationship with Phoebe in order to fulfill his father's nutty will. Phoebe had hooked up with Rand, and Carter had been forced to go to Plan B. Or was she Plan C? No way would she have been his first choice. If it weren't for the sex thing, he would never have looked twice at her.

For some inexplicable reason, he wanted her, but if she messed that up, where would that leave her? Married to a guy regretting his choice even more than Jack had.

154 / *Lucy Monroe*

Carter should have married a woman like Phoebe Alexander.

Just looking at her sister-in-law smiling and dancing with her husband, Rand, made Daisy's teeth ache. Phoebe was everything she wasn't. Well-educated and beautiful in a regal, society princess sort of way. She was also much nicer than any woman so at home in high society had a right to be. She'd congratulated Daisy and welcomed her to the family and she'd meant it.

Daisy was sure Carter's mother didn't, even if she had made an attempt to be gracious. She'd air-kissed the space beside Daisy's cheek and told her they must do lunch at the country club. Daisy had never even been inside the place and had no burning desire to do so.

Carter's lips trailed a path down Daisy's neck, and she shivered. Heaven help her, she was going to explode from the combination of excitement and fear coursing through her before they ever made it out of the elegant reception hall Carter's mother had insisted on renting for the occasion.

"Are you about ready to leave?"

The feel of Carter's breath against her neck was every bit as tantalizing as his kisses had been. "R-ready?"

"Yes, *ready*. I know I am." The subtle increase of pressure of his body against hers left no doubt exactly what he meant.

"We don't want to offend anyone by leaving too early."

"Don't worry. They'll understand."

He pulled back from her and looked down, his blue eyes sending a message that both enthralled and alarmed her. "Let's go."

It didn't take very long to say goodbye because the guest list was so small, but even so, by the time they made it to his black Jaguar, she was a wreck.

He unlocked the passenger door and helped her inside.

"No limo?" she asked. Everything else about the wedding had been so traditional.

"I don't like other people driving me."

She remembered. "Not even limo drivers?"

He waited to answer until he'd gotten inside and started the car. "Not even trained chauffeurs."

"Well, that's something to be grateful for." She couldn't imagine a life of being carted from one place to another by a paid driver, and no way was she giving up her Xterra.

He looked at her briefly before turning back to the road. "How so?"

"I'm not used to having people around me paid to do stuff I usually do. You know, like a housekeeper, or chauffeur or anything." He hadn't said anything about hiring any kind of domestic staff, and she was hoping it would stay that way.

She'd been really relieved when he suggested he move into her house. He said he really liked the way she'd done it up, and that made her feel good. She also liked knowing he didn't expect her to jump into a whole different lifestyle all at once.

Thinking along those lines, another question popped out. "Do I have to join the country club?"

"Is this about you fitting in, Daisy? Because I have to tell you, the only person you have to worry about fitting with in this marriage is me. And we're going to fit like we were made for each other."

"We aren't going to spend our whole life in the bedroom, Carter!"

He flicked her a serious glance. "I wasn't just talking about bed. I don't care if you join the country club. I'm not interested in keeping up appearances. That kind of life brought a lot of pain to my parents, and I don't want it. Daisy, *I like being with you,* and I'm not interested in you becoming someone else to try to fit into what you think our marriage should be."

His tone was almost severe, like this was a major issue for him. It was for her, too, actually.

"I'm glad. I like being with you, too, but I don't think I'll ever have much in common with your mother."

"I don't have much in common with her either. I love her, but, honey, you married me, not her."

That sounded good, but she still had doubts.

"Phoebe looked beautiful." It was a blatant fishing expedition, but she had too many jumbled thoughts fighting for supremacy in her mind to be subtle.

"Not as beautiful as the bride."

Daisy looked down at her bridal gown, trying to ignore the almost scandalous amount of cleavage on display. "It is a pretty dress."

"The woman inside is gorgeous."

"You don't have to flatter me, Carter. I know what I look like."

"Yeah, my favorite wet dream."

She gasped. "I can't believe you said that."

His laughter filled the car. "You are so naive about some things, honey. I can promise you that you were the only woman in that reception hall that got my attention today."

"That's because you're on edge about sex. You've abstained too long maybe."

"Nothing like six years."

"Yes . . . Well . . ." She cleared her throat, not knowing how to answer that.

She was already feeling the worry about that six-year drought and the lack of practical application she had to bring to the *wedding night of all wedding nights* he had planned.

"I'm pretty smart, you know?"

"You're very intelligent. Your supervisor thinks you're the best thing that ever happened to her department. She was really resistant to the idea of you moving out of it."

"Why would I move out of my department?"

"I didn't know how comfortable the wife of the owner of

the company would feel working for one of my middle managers."

"I love my job, and I'm not giving it up. That's not part of the deal, Carter."

He spared her a quick glance. "You're a rich woman now, Daisy. I'll take care of you. You don't have to work."

That's what he thought. "I will repeat: I like my job. I'm not quitting."

He laid his hand on her thigh and squeezed. "Don't get upset about it. If you want to keep working, you keep working."

It was all she could do to remember what they were talking about with his fingers now fondling her leg. They were way too close to the apex of her thighs for any sort of peace of mind.

"I can't wait to get you out of this dress, Daisy."

"About that . . ."

"About what?"

"This whole sex thing."

"Sex thing?" He choked the words out around laughter, and she groaned.

"Yes. Anyway, you know I don't have a lot of experience, but I'm smart, Carter."

"We've agreed on that point, but I'm not sure where you're going with it."

"If I don't get things right the first time, I can learn how," she said, exposing her deepest fear.

If he would just be patient, she knew she could learn to make love the way that he needed and expected.

The Jag swerved into the far right lane, then off the road, coming to an abrupt halt that sent Daisy pitching forward against her seat belt.

Carter turned his body to face her, his expression incredibly intense. "*I am not paying you to go to bed with me,* and

I don't need you performing like a paid lady of the night in my bed. Got it?"

"I didn't mean—"

But he cut her off. "I want to make love to you until you can't walk, but there isn't a right way or a wrong way for us to go about making that happen. I do not want you trying to please me like some kind of *sex client.*"

She couldn't walk right now if her life had depended on it, so he'd already achieved his goal without even touching her. Her legs had turned to jelly at the fury in his voice, the frustration emanating off him in waves and the sensual threat in his voice.

"I'm not a prostitute, and I don't see you as a sex client." Whatever that was.

His teeth ground together. "Then what's all this crap about learning how to perform the way I like it?"

"I was pretty much a failure at the sex thing before you, and, Carter, I can't be sure that I'm good at anything beyond really wild kissing. In fact, I'm not even sure that wasn't some sort of aberration brought about by six years of abstinence and however long it has been for you."

"You're worried you'll disappoint me?" His teeth were still gritted, but he didn't look quite so ferocious around the eyes.

"Yes."

"But not because you want to give me full value for my half a million dollars."

She opened her mouth, but the denial wouldn't come. He had paid five hundred thousand dollars to her so she would marry him and sleep with him. There was a small part of her that felt that kind of thing deserved at least a moderate return on the investment. It didn't make her feel like a prostitute, though, and why that should be, she didn't understand.

Neither did Carter, by the look of him.

As her silence grew, so did his anger until he erupted into cursing that would have made her brother blush. And he had been an Army Ranger.

"Carter."

He ignored her and turned back to face front, twisting the key in the ignition to start the car, only realizing it was still going when an awful grinding sound accompanied the movement. He growled out another cuss word and pulled back onto the highway with squealing tires.

"I wanted you to have options, to be able to end the marriage if you felt you had to. Not to feel trapped."

He shifted into a higher gear, and the car shot forward at a truly breathtaking speed.

Daisy clung to the door.

"I did not pay you so that you would feel the need to earn the money in my bed. I want you in my bed because you want to be there, damn it!"

"I *do* want to be there."

He acted as if she hadn't said anything, weaving through traffic with more skill than sense, and she gasped as he came particularly close to the rear bumper of another car.

"Slow down, Carter, you're scaring me."

"I'm mad."

"I can tell, but I don't want to be dead, or—" Her voice caught, and she screamed as he narrowly avoided a semi truck-trailer.

The Jag began to slow immediately. Carter went so far as to move into the right lane with the slowest-moving traffic.

"I'm sorry," he ground out. "I don't normally drive like that."

"I am, too. Sorry, that is. I'm scared of disappointing you, but it doesn't have anything to do with the money. Not really. Please believe me, Carter."

His grip on the steering wheel did not lessen, nor did his

jaw relax at all. "You have no reason to be afraid. We've already proven that we're more combustible together than a match and a stick of dynamite."

"But that was just kissing."

"It was a hell of a lot more than kissing."

She could see that he was not going to understand her. She didn't even know if she understood herself. All she did know was that a woman who had the sexual past she did, did not have unfailing confidence in her ability to please her lover.

Only time and experience would tell if her fears were justified.

The silence in the car stretched until it felt like a rubber band pulled taut, ready to snap with sharp and painful impact at anyone in its radius.

"Do you want to call it off?" she finally asked, her voice choked with the failure she could not seem to evict from her life.

"*No*. I want to make love to you so often and so long that you can't think of anything but me. Not the money. Not your insecurities. Not having to join some damn country club. Just me."

"Oh."

Neither one of them said another word on the remainder of the drive to the secluded cabin in the woods Carter had rented for their honeymoon.

He pulled up in front and cut the engine. "We're here."

"Yes."

He unbuckled his seat belt and pulled on the handle to open the door.

She grabbed his shoulder. "Carter."

He turned his head, his blue eyes dark and unfathomable. "What?"

She wanted to say, *I love you*, but knew he wouldn't believe her. How could she love a man she'd gotten to know personally only a few days ago? He didn't know about her years' long obsession. However, he could believe in her desire for him because *he wanted her, too.*

"I want to be here. I want to be with you."

He pulled her hand from his shoulder, but he didn't fling it away as she was half expecting him to do. Instead, he lifted it to his mouth and kissed her palm.

Her eyes filled with tears. "Thank you."

She didn't know why she'd said it, but she felt as if the kiss had been a benediction, one she'd desperately needed.

His eyes closed, and he kissed the tingling flesh of her palm again. Then he let go and opened his eyes. "Come on. I don't think I can wait much longer."

She wasn't sure how he could want her so much when he had been so furious only moments before, but his tone was one of absolute certainty. She had the feeling that if they didn't get inside in the next five minutes, they were going to end up consummating their marriage in the passenger seat of his Jag.

Chapter Seven

Carter was there when she pushed the door open. He lifted her out of the low-slung car, and he swung her up in his arms.

"I believe tradition says I carry you over the threshold."

She clasped her hands behind his neck. "I'm all for tradition, Mr. Sloane."

"Good, Mrs. Sloane." He said the words with a significance she didn't get, but she didn't dwell on it for long.

She was too awed by her surroundings. The large log cabin had a sunken living room with a fireplace and acres and acres of windows that looked out over a burbling stream and tons of deciduous trees that were all turning color for autumn.

It was the most beautiful thing she'd ever seen.

"It's perfect," she breathed.

She looked up at him, ready to say something else, but her voice stalled in her throat at the hot look in his eyes.

The incredible view, the luxury of the cabin, every detail of her surroundings ceased to matter.

The only thing she could see was the man she'd just married. The only thing she could feel was the heat of his body next to hers. The only thing she could smell was the scent of her lover. The only thing she could hear was the sound of his breathing, shallow and short. The only thing she could taste was the tang of desire on her tongue.

Her world had shrunk to include only him, and her own breathing sped up right along with her pulse.

She said the one thing that made sense right at that moment. "Kiss me, Carter, please."

Insistent, masculine lips covered hers, branding her with a heat that went clear to her soul.

She belonged to this man.

Completely and without reservation.

His tongue teased her lips, and she parted them for him, hungry for his possession of her mouth. He gave it. She sucked on his tongue, sliding hers against it, kissing with a passionate intensity that only this man drew from her.

It ignited a carnality in his kiss that blew her thought processes to smithereens.

She was unaware of him letting go of her legs, but suddenly she was standing, and his hands were busy on the tiny buttons that went down the back of her dress. His mouth continued to devour hers, and she tore at the studs holding his tuxedo shirt together. The stupid things would not let go and she was in danger of ripping the fine linen, when he drew away from her.

"Let me do it."

She didn't argue, just stood and gloried in the sight of Carter's body as it was revealed bit by bit to her gaze. The tie went first, sailing off in the direction of the coffee table. Then the studs. One by one, he took them from his shirt until it hung loose.

She stepped forward, her own gown slipping down to reveal the demibra she'd worn because he asked her to.

He sucked in air, and his gaze zeroed in on her breasts and stayed there, while she pushed his shirt off his shoulders, glad he'd taken his coat off when they got in the car earlier.

She reached down for the front of his pants, and his big body jolted as if he'd touched a live electrical current.

She felt like one.

The fastening and zipper on his pants were a lot easier for her fumbling fingers, and pretty soon she was pushing those down his thighs as well. He toed off his shoes and socks and stepped out of his pants with an economy of movement that impressed her.

His boxers tented in front, the waistband actually pulling away from his body a little from the pressure his hard penis put on the fabric. He was big.

Which should have made her more nervous, but it didn't. She happened to believe they *had* been made to fit together and somehow it was going to work.

She felt wet enough to make his entry smooth if not instantaneous.

Prickly shivers ran down the backs of her thighs at the wild look in his eyes.

"Take off your dress."

It was a command, plain and simple, but his tone carried something more. A desperation that touched her heart and made her body melt like heated honey on the inside.

Just this once, she would obey.

She lowered her arms to her sides and let the antique lace gown slide down her body and fall to the floor in a heap of cream satin around her feet.

She moved toward him again, stepping over the gown, but he shook his head.

"I want to see you."

She felt the heat of a blush crawl up her body, or was that the heat of his gaze?

Whatever it was, it felt as though she'd stepped into a dry sauna, and she could barely breathe. "You just want to look?"

He nodded. "I've been fantasizing about this all day."

She shouldn't be so shocked. She'd had her share of day-dreams about him wearing less than he was right now, though none of those dreams had done his actual body justice.

He was beautifully toned and proportioned in a way to stop a woman's heart . . . or capture it.

His blue gaze roamed over her in a way that made her feel touched everywhere it rested. "Rand told me Phoebe has a thing for sexy lingerie. It's a habit I think I could learn to like in a wife."

"Is that a hint?" The words barely made it past the dry Sahara of her throat.

He shook his head. "Nah. I like buying it for you too much. I was just commenting."

"Oh," she squeaked as his look zeroed in on the triangle of satin covering her now-damp curls between her thighs.

"Turn around. I want to see your ass."

"*What?*"

He let his eyes travel up her body until they met her own. "You want me to."

She did, which shocked her to death, but the idea of him looking at her with such blatant male appreciation was a major turn-on. Mesmerized by the sexual power radiating off of him and her own inexplicable reaction to it, she turned.

"You were made for a G-string."

"My butt's too big."

"Not from where I'm standing."

Oh, goodness. His voice brought a burst of warmth between her legs. She heard a whisper of movement, and then his fingers brushed the place where her cheeks came together.

She turned her head to see him.

He wasn't looking anywhere near her face. "You're perfect. A masterpiece of sensual beauty."

She didn't know what to say. No one had ever looked at her like that before, or thought those things, much less said them.

"If I told you to bend over, would you do it?"

Her heart stopped beating and then sped up as if she'd taken a shot of adrenaline. "Maybe if you asked nicely," she croaked out.

"Would you please bend over, Daisy?"

The whiskey roughness of his voice caressed her insides while her body moved to obey the plea in his voice.

She bent forward, letting her hands rest for added balance on the back of the white sofa facing the windows.

"Spread your legs a little."

She didn't move.

"*Please.*"

She smiled to herself and let her feet separate about four inches. She wasn't sure where this teasing wanton had come from, but Daisy liked the heady sense of feminine power Carter's obvious desire was giving her.

Husky male laughter met the movement. "You little tease. Give me at least six more inches."

She looked back over her shoulder again, wanting to see his reaction as she did as he asked. She widened her stance, bending her knees slightly. It was a totally sexual pose, but it made her feel warm and sultry inside, not cheap.

His jaw set in granite-hard lines, while his hands clenched at his sides.

"Stay like that," he commanded in a gravelly voice.

"For how long?"

"Until I tell you to move."

Was this part of giving her the wedding night of all wedding nights? It was certainly pushing her beyond where she'd ever gone before in her sexuality. He was hardly touching her at all, and yet she felt as though what they were doing was more intimate than anything she'd ever done with her first husband. Including the act of intercourse.

Carter would make her glad she cooperated, she was sure of it.

"All right."

His face took on the cast of a predator, and his smile was more the baring of teeth than anything else. "Good."

He came closer until his straining erection rubbed up against her bottom through the silk of his boxers. "Face the front and don't look at me again unless I tell you to."

That wasn't a problem. Darkness had fallen outside, turning the wall of windows into a mirror through which she could watch her husband do whatever it was he planned to do to her. And she watched in utter fascination as he took off his last remaining bit of clothing, leaving his masculine flesh open to her hungry gaze. She didn't get to look long, though.

His fingers clamped onto her hips, and he rubbed his now naked hardness against her backside, up and down the center, teasing them both with the touch that tantalized but did not deliver.

"Do you like that?"

"Yes."

He did it some more until she was straining to move against that hold on her hips. Her arms folded, and she dropped forward until her forearms rested on the back of the couch. She wasn't looking in the mirrored window any longer. She was just feeling, and what she felt was driving her insane.

He pulled back, and she whimpered.

"Hush, honey. Trust me."

"Yessss . . . ," she hissed out. She did trust him.

She felt a gentle kiss right at the base of her neck. Then one baby kiss after another until he'd worked his way down her spine. By the time he reached her bottom, she was shaking and could barely stand. Would have fallen in a heap on the floor, in fact, if she hadn't been leaning on the sofa.

He used his tongue and lips in shocking, pleasurable ways on her backside that had her groaning and begging for his possession.

"You want me inside you?" His breath caressed her most feminine flesh.

"Yes!"

"Your wish is my command."

And then she felt him inside her. Wet. Slippery and oh, so talented, his tongue penetrated her labia with one thrust after another. Completely abandoned to her desire, she pressed back against his face, seeking greater penetration.

He increased the pace of his thrusts and then varied them with swirls around her clitoris, followed by more thrusts, followed by more clitoral stimulation. The seemingly never ending cycle drove her beyond reason as pleasure built upon pleasure, radiating from the core of her body outward.

When his hands came around to her front and cupped her breasts, she cried out. When he squeezed her nipples between his fingers, she felt it inside her womb.

The pleasure became unbearable, and her knees buckled from a heart-shattering orgasm that left her throat raw from screaming.

His hold on her front stopped her from pitching forward. He pulled back, so she landed on his hard thighs instead of hanging like a limp rag over the back of the couch when her muscles gave out.

Hands so gentle they felt like billowing silk against her skin brushed over her breasts, down her stomach and along her trembling thighs.

"You're so perfect for me." His words were filled with the same awe she felt.

She turned her face into his neck. *"You're* perfect."

His laughter rumbled against her back. "Not perfect, but definitely in need."

She could feel his erection pressing against her. If she shifted up just a little, he would be able to penetrate her, and she wanted that as much as he did.

She tried to make the movement, but he held her in place. "Not yet, Daisy."

"*I don't want to wait anymore, Carter.*"

One of his arms slid under knees and the other around her back, shifting her into a cradle against his body. He stood up without any visible effort and smiled down at her.

"I want to be inside you, too, but I think I must be a little old-fashioned."

If she had just one more iota of energy, she would have laughed at that. Old-fashioned? Him? The man who had turned her into a raving wanton woman? Not likely.

"I want to see your face the first time I come inside you." He looked so serious, so intent, that her heart contracted.

She didn't know how old-fashioned that was, but it certainly was sweet. "I'd like that."

He carried her into the bedroom, her shoes falling off on the way. The thumps they made as they dropped from her feet only barely registered. She got an impression of lots of white and big wooden furniture before she found herself flat on her back with Carter looming over her.

"I need a glove. Will you put it on me?"

"A glove?"

He was already leaning over her and grabbing something from under one of the pillows. When he came back with a foil packet, comprehension donned.

"You want me to put your condom on you?" She'd never done that before.

He reared up on his knees, his hard-on bobbing in front of him in swollen urgency. "You don't have to do it."

But she wanted to. She put her hand out for the packet, and he handed it to her with fingers that shook.

She pushed herself up into a sitting position with her thighs spread around him.

It left her exposed and feeling very sexy.

Her breasts were spilling over the demicups of her bra, and she still wore the stay-ups and thong. Not that the tiny strings holding the small triangle of satin in front of her mound were any deterrent to him at all. He'd shown that out in the great room.

She reached out and touched him, just the tip, and a drop of pre-come appeared on his head. She put her finger on it and then put it to her lips and tasted. She'd never tasted a man like this before. It was odd, salty and sweet at the same time.

His long and low groan had her looking at his face. His features were etched with pain.

"Did I hurt you?"

"No, you didn't hurt me, but if you don't get the condom on me soon, we're going to have kids sooner than later."

"I want children with you, Carter, but not just yet."

He nodded, apparently incapable of further speech.

She didn't want to talk right now either. Putting the condom on him was easier than she expected, though the fit was really tight. He moaned with each stroke of her fingers, and as soon as it was on, he pressed her back into the bed.

"Forgive me, Daisy."

"What for?"

Even as the words were leaving her mouth, he was ripping the satin thong from her body and tossing it aside. "I want to see and feel all of you."

And then he was doing just that. Feeling her anyway.

He spread her lips and pressed his penis into her opening. It was tight, but she was very slick from her excitement and her climax, and she felt nothing but good sensations as he pushed farther inside.

"Come on, baby, I know you can take all of me."

She wasn't so sure about that. It didn't hurt, but she was full. How could there possibly be room for more?

He hooked his elbows under her knees and lifted, spreading her legs farther apart and opening her to him in a way that left her completely vulnerable to his possession.

"I need you to relax."

"It feels too good to relax." Her eyes closed in ecstatic pleasure as he moved, caressing sensitive inner tissues.

"Please, Daisy. Concentrate on opening yourself to me."

She tried, and somehow, bit by bit, he rocked himself into her until their pelvic bones met.

Completely filled, she was pinned to the bed and unable to move so much as a centimeter. "Now what?"

"Now I make you mine."

Chapter Eight

Carter had never felt anything so incredible.

She was so tight, so wet, and so swollen around him.

So perfect.

He leaned down and slammed his mouth over hers as he started to move his hips. What he felt was too elemental to express with a slow and gentle buildup. She didn't seem to mind.

Her arms locked around his neck, and she returned his passion, kiss for searing kiss.

Her position didn't give her much room for movement, but she tried, straining toward him and welcoming his increasingly strong thrusts with feminine sounds of encouragement. Her eraser-hard nipples grazed against his chest as her breasts shook from the force of his thrusting. He loved the feeling, but he wanted to see it, too.

Rearing up on his arms, he slammed into her with passion he could no longer contain.

"Yes, Carter, oh, yes, please. Don't stop!"

"I couldn't," he admitted with what little breath he had left in his lungs.

Her head thrashed from side to side, pulling her long hair out of its elaborate do for the wedding.

The picture of abandonment to passion she made excited him beyond the point of rational thought. Her nipples were berry red in their excitement and so hard, they pointed straight out. The creamy flesh of her breasts shook with each movement of his body over hers, just begging to be held and caressed.

With a feral growl, he lowered his head and took one of the tempting red morsels into his mouth. Sucked it. Bit it and then kissed it when she made an animal sound of her own. He turned his head and did the same thing to her other nipple, satisfaction coursing through him.

She was his.

He could touch her like this for the rest of their lives.

Finally, after four years. He was holding the phantom that had haunted him in his arms.

And that reality was driving him right over the edge.

"You've got to get to it or I'm going without you."

And he couldn't do that. He wanted to share it with her.

She bowed under him, pressing her pelvis against his own with each thrust. He gyrated his hips to increase the friction around her clitoris and watched with male pride as her eyes glazed over, her mouth opened on a silent scream and she came. Again. This time with him inside her and her inner muscles holding him so tightly that he felt as if he really was a part of her body.

Then the pleasure at the base of his shaft seemed to explode up it, and he came inside her like a river bursting through a dam. Sensations flooded him. Overwhelming emotions that had no name, but filled his heart to bursting.

Want. Need. Desire. They were all there, but so was an inescapable tenderness. *I love you, Daisy*, his mind screamed as his throat let loose a raw shout of triumphant gratification.

Afterward, he collapsed on top of her, the softness of her body an irresistible lure to rest for muscles that had lost their ability to function. Her arms fell away from him, and her legs dropped limply to the bed.

They stayed that way for a long time, neither one of them speaking.

Then she turned her head, just a little, but enough to press her lips into his neck. "That was the most beautiful experience of my life."

"Me, too, Daisy. Me, too."

The words his mind had screamed earlier were on the tip of his tongue, but he could not make them come out. Not yet.

It took a while, but he managed to gather enough strength to get up and take care of the condom, come back and tuck them both under the covers before falling into an exhausted sleep, more sated in mind, heart and body than he had been in his entire life.

Carter came awake slowly, unsure at first if he was really holding Daisy, or if it was another dream.

But the warm and womanly body in his arms was too real to be a delusion.

And what they'd shared earlier had been too amazing to be just sex. He'd had sex before, many times, but tonight was the first time he'd ever made love to a woman in the most literal sense of the words.

For years, he'd believed himself as incapable of that all-encompassing emotion as his father, only to discover in the midst of the most mind blowing intimacy of his life that love wasn't outside his nature after all.

He loved Daisy, and it was such a bone-deep emotion, he knew he could never dismiss it or her from his life.

The only problem was, he had no idea what she felt.

She'd let him make love to her with a freedom that encompassed his deepest fantasies. She had allowed him to find

176 / Lucy Monroe

pleasure in her body and to give her pleasure in a way he was almost positive she'd never had before. But had she done that because of the money, or because she felt something for him like he felt for her?

He couldn't believe that Daisy would be motivated by the money to love him like she'd done.

Not the woman he'd come to know through her personnel file, talking to her coworkers and spending time with her.

He didn't know why she'd married him, but he was almost positive it wasn't because he'd paid her to do so.

She'd had a rotten sex life in her first marriage, and he could almost believe that she'd been willing to marry him because he gave her something she'd never had sexually before. Satisfaction.

But that didn't ring true either.

A woman like Daisy would need to feel something powerful in her heart for her body to respond the way it did.

Moonlight spilled in through a cathedral-style bedroom window, and he could see the gentle curve of her lips as well as the soft expression of her face in sleep.

Total innocence.

Incomparable beauty.

His Daisy.

He wanted to know what she felt. Needed desperately to know.

He reached out and touched her cheek, rubbing his finger up and down until she started to stir.

Daisy woke to the sensation of butterfly wings brushing against her face.

Her eyes fluttered open to the sight of Carter leaning over her, an incredibly fervent expression on his face.

She smiled. "Hi."

His hand shifted to cup her cheek. "Hi."

She slid one leg between his. "Mmm . . . that's nice."

His eyes closed. "Very nice."

She reached down and brushed his male flesh. It twitched at her touch, and he groaned, but then his hand caught her wrist.

"Stop for a second." His eyes were open again.

"Why?" She could tell he liked it, so she didn't feel even a smidgen of rejection.

"I need to ask you a question."

She leaned forward and kissed the muscled wall of his chest. "Then ask it."

"Did you make love to me like that because you were trying to give me full value for that damn money or because you love me?"

She went completely still. "Isn't there an Option C?"

"I don't know. Is there?"

She moved back a little so she could see his face. The semi-darkness could not hide the vulnerability in his expression.

"I didn't come to your bed because you paid me to do it."

"You kept harping on the fact I was paying you to sleep with me."

She bit her lip, then sighed. "Well, you see, your motives weren't necessarily mine, if you know what I mean."

"I hope I do. Explain it to me, just in case." He had the air of a man hanging on her every word, and she really didn't want to mess this up.

"You offered me money to do something I wanted to do. So, it didn't matter you were offering the money except that it made me feel sort of racy and exciting when I'd always been a boring little nobody."

"*You are not boring.* You're the most exciting woman I have ever known."

That deserved another kiss, so she gave it. "Thank you."

"So, why did you want to marry me? Was it the sex?"

"You're pretty good at that."

"That's not what I asked."

"Why are you asking?" she demanded in an attempt at

stalling the inevitable. She was going to have to admit she loved him, and part of her didn't mind at all.

He'd told her it would be all right if she came to love him, so she had to assume he wouldn't mind that she'd loved him all along.

"I love you, Daisy, and it's killing me to think you don't feel the same way."

Her lungs froze right between taking a breath and letting it out. "Wh . . ." She couldn't make the word come out.

"Daisy?"

The bedroom was getting really dark, and then he was pounding on her back, and she started breathing again. She gasped in air and let it out several times before she got the question out she'd meant to ask. *"What?"*

"I love you, and I'm not sure how you feel about me, but I'll be damned if I expected the news to make you stop breathing in shock."

Tears filled her eyes, and she hugged him as tight as she could, tiny sobs escaping between kisses to his chest, his neck, his chin, his mouth and his cheeks.

Two big hands locked onto either side of her head. "Does this mean you're happy about how I feel?"

She laughed. "Yes." How could he doubt it? She went back to kissing him.

He caught her face again. "And you love me, too?"

She sat straight up and looked down at him, this man whom she now, finally, believed she could have for a lifetime. "Oh, yes. I love you. I've loved you forever, it seems. Jack used to accuse me of mooning over you, the unattainable man. I tried not to, when I was married, but after he died, you were everything my dreams were made of."

He sat up, too, his big body gleaming in the moonlight. "How could you love me? You didn't know me."

"Didn't I? You were right when you said your life is an open book to the town of New Hope. I knew about your childhood, how cold your mother is and how careful you've always been with her. I knew about the way you treated your jerk of a dad with respect and the way you were always looking for ways to improve the employees' lot with the company."

"And then I met you. Four years ago and every daydream I had had about this ideal man coalesced around a reality that devastated me. I cried when I read about your engagement to Phoebe. I ached with missing you when you moved to New York, even though I only saw you occasionally as it was."

"I left because of you."

She couldn't comprehend what he'd just said.

"I broke my engagement with Phoebe because I wanted you so much I woke up in a cold sweat at night after dreaming about you. I thought I was fickle like my father, that I wasn't capable of love. So, I left, to protect Phoebe from marrying a man who would hurt her in the end and to protect you from an affair with the same guy."

Her heart contracted with pain for what he'd believed about himself. "But you came back."

"It didn't go away. The ache, or the wanting, and being in New York didn't make any difference. I figured that even if I couldn't do love, I knew I could do fidelity. I was already doing it."

She couldn't believe what she was hearing. "You couldn't have wanted me that much." Her voice cracked on tears that insisted on rolling down her cheeks.

"You're right." He pulled her into his lap and cradled her against him, brushing the tears from her cheeks with his fingers. "It wasn't just want. It was love. I don't understand it, but I know it's real."

She leaned into him, inhaling his scent, soaking in his warmth. "Oh, yes, it's real."

"A forever kind of real."

She leaned up to kiss him, and that led to more touching, which led to pleasure that left her in tears all over again.

Later, curled into his body, her legs entwined with his and on the verge of sleep, she laid her hand against his heart. "Forever."

Colton's Story

Chapter One

Somebody had stuck a vise on Colton Denning's temples, and it was so tight, he thought his head might explode.

Idiot.

He never drank, but had that stopped him from finishing off an entire bottle of champagne by himself? No, it had not.

Now he had to live with the consequences.

A head that wanted somebody to shoot it and put it out of its misery. A mouth that tasted as if it had been stuffed with sawdust used to soak up a wrestler's sweat. Okay, that image had been a little too graphic. His stomach roiled, and his throat convulsed.

He forced one eyelid open. He was facedown on a bed. That was good. The last thing he remembered was watching the follies in the showroom at his Vegas hotel. At least he'd made it back to his room. Now, if he could just make it to the bathroom before he lost whatever was in his stomach . . .

With an unmanly groan he would never have let another person hear, he shoved one leg off the side of the bed. Then the other one. Using his arms as leverage, he pushed upward. If he couldn't make it off of his knees, at least he could crawl to the bathroom.

Bleary eyes took in the details of his bed. The bedspread

was hanging off the end of the mattress, and the covers were a mess, really lumpy.

Make that extremely lumpy.

The shock of what he was seeing sent him staggering to his feet. He reeled backward, then staggered forward again until his shins ran right into the side of the bed. He rubbed his hand over his eyes, but it didn't erase what he saw.

A woman.

A naked, very voluptuous woman was in his bed.

Long, chestnut hair covered her averted face, but he didn't need to see her features to be absolutely certain he didn't know her. Because the blankets *did not* cover her body. Perfectly formed breasts with wine rose tips peaked at him from amidst the white linen. Her arms were thrown above her head in sleepy abandon. The sheet and blanket that barely covered her belly were twisted around her shapely calves and did nothing to hide the feminine curls at the apex of her very toned thighs.

Aw, hell. With a body like that, she had to be a showgirl.

He didn't date showgirls. He wasn't big on dating, period, but when he did date, he took out women who thought flamboyant was wearing a red sweater set instead of brown. Nothing like his mother, Moonbeam, the original flower child who'd never grown out of her tie-dye T-shirts and bangle bracelets. And definitely nothing like this gorgeous creature in his bed.

Of course, she hadn't been a date.

She'd been a one-night stand. Another never for him.

Even as his dick responded to the sight of her oh-so-perfect body, his stomach clenched at the idiocy of going to bed with a stranger. His initial reason for forcing his body from the bed made itself known again. He spun on his heel, which sent the vise on his temples into a pulsating mode, but he didn't care. He had to get to the bathroom.

He made it, shutting the door with a jerky movement. Afterward, he brushed his teeth and drank several glasses of water from the tap, downing some aspirin with one of them.

He leaned against the counter, refusing to even glance in the mirror at the fool who'd taken an unknown woman to bed and risked his life for a night of sex he couldn't even remember. He felt as though he'd been run over by one of his excavation units, and what was he supposed to say to the woman lying in his bed? He didn't even know her name.

No doubt, she'd really get a kick out of learning that fact. It suddenly occurred to him that he had no desire to stick around for an awkward morning after.

Had his bathroom ablutions woken the woman in his bed? He snuck a peak around the partially closed bathroom door.

She'd turned onto her side, exposing luscious, round cheeks he wished he could remember touching because sure as certain, he wasn't going to be touching them again. Her soft, slow breathing indicated she was still asleep.

He quietly snuck back into the main room and started searching for the clothes he'd been wearing the night before. He found his slacks in a pile under some spangly white thing. Her costume. It didn't look as if it covered up much more than the sheet was doing this morning.

He tossed it aside and grabbed the pants, his knees about buckling with relief as several opened condom packets scattered to the floor. At least they'd practiced safe sex. Having no memory of the previous night after his third glass of champagne, he had to assume he owed the woman in his bed thanks for making sure they had used protection.

He grabbed the rest of his clothes off the floor and tossed them into his duffel bag with the others he'd packed yesterday. He'd planned to get an early start on his trip to Mexico this morning. He was supposed to meet his brothers on Luna

Island in three days, and he still had to confirm delivery of the exploratory mining equipment to Las Playas del Blanco and arrange its transport to the island.

He dragged on a pair of tan Dockers and a T-shirt. He would have to forgo a shower. No way was he risking waking the woman up with the sound of running water.

He'd grabbed his shaving kit from the bathroom, slung his duffel bag over his shoulder and had his hand on the door handle when he stopped. Okay, so maybe it had been a one-night stand, but could he just leave her like that? Naked and in his bed. She deserved a note or something.

Considering the number of condoms they'd used, he had to figure she'd given him a heck of a night, even if he couldn't remember it. He went back to the desk under the window and pulled out a sheet of hotel stationery.

It took him several minutes to decide what to write, but finally he had it down and was on his way out the door.

He stopped at the front desk and paid the exorbitant fee Vegas hotels charged for keeping his room a night longer than his reservation. He didn't want her being kicked out of bed by housekeeping later that afternoon.

It was the best he could do for her.

Fayre kicked the flat tire on her lime green Volkswagen Beetle.

She was going to kill him. When she caught up with that too damn sexy, good-for-nothing, lying, leave-a-woman-sleeping-in-bed-while-he-snuck-out creep, she was going to murder him. Slowly. And she was going to enjoy doing it.

But murder and mayhem had to wait while she changed the tire on her little car, the hot sun making her oversized T-shirt and crop pants feel like an Eskimo parka.

Oh, she was going to make him pay.

She really was.

Right after he explained how he could just walk out like that after all the things he'd said.

A crack of almost hysterical laughter echoed around her. Why even bother asking? Mr. Colton Denning had just been another frickin' bad choice in men. The kind she excelled at.

When was she going to learn?

But, damn it, he'd seemed so sincere.

She didn't trust men, never, not anymore. So, how had she let herself fall for his line? He'd *seemed* so sincere. He'd *seemed* different than the other creeps who saw her body and nothing else.

He hadn't been, and it had hurt more than she'd thought possible to hurt anymore. She should be inured to that kind of thing by now, the love her, leave her crap. So, how had he gotten under her skin and right into her heart?

She'd believed his line about love at first sight because she'd felt the same thing.

Only she hadn't. Oh, what she'd felt had been real enough. Hence the pain in her heart that would not go away, but he hadn't felt anything more than the twitching of his oversized dick in his custom-tailored pants.

The sound of another car coming on the deserted highway sent her thoughts scattering. She spun around to look, shielding her eyes from the sun, even though she was wearing her Donna Karan sunglasses. It was an old rattle-trap truck, too many colors to distinguish which had been the original. Pulling to a stop behind her car, the engine shuddered to a halt.

Fear coursed through her. She was a woman alone on a deserted road in Mexico, and her Spanish was only marginally better than her grasp of nuclear physics. She read dictionaries for pleasure, but they were in English.

The sun glared off the windshield, blocking her from seeing the driver, and her body went tense in preparation for flight or fight. But it wasn't the driver's door that opened first.

The passenger door banged open, and two small children tumbled out of the truck cab. They were followed by an obviously pregnant woman who had Fayre's immediate empathy.

Finally, the driver's door opened, and a stocky Mexican man stepped out. He smiled at Fayre, said something to his wife that made *her* smile and something to his children that sent them rushing to the back of the truck. He walked over to his wife and took her arm, helping her walk with all the solicitude of gentle and obvious love.

Fayre's eyes smarted with tears for no good reason she could think of.

The two came over to where she stood next to a half-jacked-up car and her spare tire. "I help you, señorita?"

On a normal day, she would have refused his help, saying she could do it herself. But this wasn't a normal day, and she offered the tire jack to him without a single argument and a heartfelt, "Thank you."

He nodded, smiled again and finished jacking up her little car. It looked like he knew what he was doing, so she left him to it.

"You go to Puerto Vallarta?" the woman asked, naming a city popular with tourists farther south on the coast.

Fayre forced her normally mobile mouth into a smile. "No. I'm going to Luna Island."

"Is pretty place."

Fayre wouldn't know. All she did know was that was where the owner of Denning Mining Operations had gone, and she was determined to track the snake down.

However, she smiled again and nodded.

The children ran up, offering Fayre a piece of fruit. She knew to refuse would offend the small family, so she accepted, but then pulled some Cokes and other snacks from her food store in the small trunk of her car to share with them. The kids were ecstatic, and watching them brought the first real grin to her face in days.

A half an hour later, she was again behind the wheel of her car, and the Mexican family was on its way.

Now, that was a man. He stopped to help a woman in distress, took care of his pregnant wife and was tender with his children. He was not some slimy toad who talked a woman into his bed and then dumped her in the morning with a note on the hotel stationery no less. Frickin' cheap and uninspired, that's what Colton Denning was.

Chapter Two

Seated at the small table in the back of the Las Playas del Blanco Taverna, Colton sipped at his coffee while he waited for his weekly supplies to be loaded onto his boat.

The coffee was bitter and lukewarm, but he hadn't had so much as a beer since the disaster in Vegas.

The woman haunted his dreams, and he had a sneaking suspicion that he was reliving the wild night in his sleeping fantasies. If that was the case, he was the biggest fool that had ever walked God's green earth for leaving her behind without so much as a goodbye.

Even if his dreams were nothing related to what really happened, his conscience ate at him when he thought of her waking up to nothing but a note and an empty hotel room.

He should have stuck around, no matter how uncomfortable it would have been. Moonbeam would be appalled if she knew he'd treated a woman like that.

His mother might live wild in a lot of ways, but she'd raised him to respect the opposite sex and protect them when at all possible. He'd done very little of that with the woman he'd left behind.

If he could remember her name, he would have called her to apologize, or maybe sent her flowers in care of the follies.

Something. If he could even remember her face, he would make plans to go back to Vegas and find her to tell her he was sorry in person. Hell, he might do it anyway.

He knew three things about her. She was a showgirl, she danced in the follies at his hotel and she was a natural brunette . . . or was that shade of chestnut considered a red-head? Anyway, he knew what color her hair was.

He knew what her ass looked like, too, and he'd give an awful lot to see it again, but her face remained a mystery. Even in his dreams.

And it bothered him.

He looked up as the doors to the taverna swung inward and a woman walked in. She was tall, easily five-ten, but that was about all he could really tell about her. She'd camouflaged her figure behind a baggy T-shirt that hung down to her thighs and loose-fitting crop pants. A pair of designer sunglasses hid her eyes, and a baseball cap covered her hair, which was scraped back into a ponytail away from a face that said the word in cranky.

She looked ready to do violence.

He wondered which of the poor fools in the taverna had pissed off the pale-faced Amazon.

Her head swiveled from side to side as she scanned the room, but before her gaze reached him, one of the men sitting at the bar got up and approached her. Garcia.

Every bar had to have a badass, and at the Las Playas del Blanco Taverna, Garcia was it. He steered a clear path around Colton. Most of the men did, but Colton had seen the man in action, and he didn't have a good feeling about what was going to go down here.

Garcia said something coarse and suggestive to the woman in Spanish. The other men around him snickered.

It didn't help that they were far enough into rural Mexico for a lot of old-world beliefs to still be a big part of the local culture. Like the idea that nice girls didn't travel alone.

The woman looked at Garcia. "I don't speak Spanish."

Her husky voice affected Colton like no woman had in the six weeks since he'd left Las Vegas.

Garcia laid his hand on her arm, stepping closer to her. "No talk, *que bueno*, señorita. I not want to talk either."

He was tall for a Mexican, but he still didn't quite meet her eye to eye. Not that that seemed to bother the guy. He was intent on proving his reputation.

She tried to shake his hand off her arm, but his grip tightened, and she winced.

Colton came to his feet without thought, and the men around him scooted backward. He was used to such a reaction to his size. He usually found it amusing. Right now, nothing was funny, though. Not with the woman starting to look scared and the men in the bar taking on the appearance of a pack of jackals.

"I'm here looking for my husband."

Colton's teeth ground together. The idiot should have known better than to send his wife into a Mexican bar without him. Even during the day, it was a bad idea.

Garcia grabbed her other arm and pulled her closer to him. "Maybe you come to the wrong place. All you find here is me."

The guy's English was pretty good, but his manners were rotten.

"Let her go."

Colton didn't expect his words to have much impact. Most of the guys in Las Playas del Blanco were good men, but with a badass like Garcia, there was no point in attempting reason. Maybe a couple of hours ago, before he'd consumed enough whiskey to turn his eyes red, but not now.

From what Colton could tell, the guy had been drinking since morning. He'd sure as certain gotten more and more belligerent over the past hour Colton had been in the taverna.

Garcia didn't turn. "You stay out of this, gringo."

"That's not going to happen."

The woman's head turned toward him when he spoke the second time. "You!" She'd been looking frightened; now she looked mad enough to take Garcia down to his toenails. *"Let me go."*

She didn't shout, but if Colton had been Garcia, he would have obeyed. The woman sounded deadly.

Garcia wasn't that smart. "I no think so. You are a pretty soft woman." He caressed her arms. "Maybe I like to feel some more of your softness."

"I told you, I'm here to see my husband." Then her knee came up at the same time as her arms came out in a classic windmill breaking his hold. She brought both hands down in a simultaneous slap on Garcia's ears.

He crumpled to the floor, cussing in Spanish as much as his labored breath would let him. He didn't even try to get up, but writhed in pain on the dirty floor. She must have gotten him a good one in the nuts.

Some of his friends moved as if to touch the woman, and Colton gave them a look that dared them to do it.

They backed off.

She didn't even notice. She wasn't looking at Garcia any longer either. Her entire attention was fixed on Colton.

"You said you came to meet your husband." For some reason he really hated saying those words. "Maybe I can help you find him. What's his name?"

She might be the wife of one of his engineers. No one had said anything about having a wife join them, but she might have decided to surprise her husband.

She whipped her sunglasses off her face. Green eyes the color of perfectly cut emeralds glared at him as if he was lower than a snake's belly. "That's not funny."

"I wasn't trying to be funny, ma'am. I'd like to help you find your husband."

"What, don't you think a Vegas marriage license is legal?"

This was getting weird. "I'm not sure—"

Her hand came up over her mouth, and her throat convulsed. She gasped in air. "I need a bathroom."

He didn't think twice about the wisdom of his actions, but swung her up in his arms and headed out of the bar. The single toilet bathroom in the back would have made her nausea worse, not better. There was a stream that ran behind the taverna all the way to the beach. He carried her there, his long legs eating up the distance.

They made it to the stream in the nick of time.

He held her while she was sick, crooning stupid stuff about how she was going to be okay and that it would feel better in a little bit. It just seemed like the right thing to do.

Though he was silently cursing her moronic husband who hadn't been in Las Playas del Blanco to meet her when she arrived. When she finished, he ripped open one of the premoistened wipes he'd kept in his pockets since coming to Mexico and washed her face.

"I know you want to rinse your mouth out, but the stream isn't safe. I'll take you to my boat. I've got bottled water and something to settle your stomach." And he'd find out where the heck her absentee husband was.

She nodded, but didn't attempt to speak. Her face was the color of the white beaches the town had been named for, and her breathing was way too shallow for his liking.

He didn't give her the option of walking, but picked her up again and headed toward the docks.

When they reached his boat, the supplies were loaded, and one of the men from town was waiting for Colton to sign the approval slip and pay him.

He nodded toward the man to tell him to wait and carried her inside his cabin. He laid her down on the bed.

Her eyes flared with alarm.

"I'll be back in a little bit, and we can go about finding
your husband. Just rest and get your breath back right now."

Her eyes went all squinty, but then she seemed to deflate
and turned her head away. "All right."

He felt wrong about leaving her, but he had a man waiting
for him. "Listen, what's your husband's name? Maybe he's in
town right now."

She turned on her side away from him, like a wounded animal seeking to minimize its vulnerability. "Go away."

Damn it, he could not leave her like this. He leaned over
the bed and laid his big hand on her shoulder. Her bones felt
fragile. "Tell me what's wrong, honey." He'd never called a
woman by an endearment in his life, but it slipped out, feeling
too natural considering she was a married woman. "Maybe I
can help."

Not that there was a whole lot he could do if she'd picked
up a stomach bug from drinking tainted water. It would just
have to run its course.

She curled up into a tighter ball, and her shoulders shook
as if she was crying.

He'd never felt so helpless in his entire life. He was the go-
to guy, the responsible one. He fixed things for people, and
here was this woman lying on his bed, crying as though her
heart was broken, and he didn't know a damn thing to do to
fix it.

"Please, just tell me your husband's name. I'll get him. I
promise." He'd drag the man to his boat by the scruff of his
neck if that's what it took.

She mumbled something into the pillow.

"What did you say?"

She lifted her head, tear-drenched eyes accusing him with
such impact, he almost believed he was the sorry bastard responsible for her plight.

"M-my husband's n-name is . . ." Her voice trailed off

into a sob. Her entire body shook, the hurting in her eyes tearing at his own soul. "C-Colton Denning."

Then she turned on her side again, dismissing him with her body language as effectively as if she'd flipped him off.

How had she known his name, and why was she so pissed at *him?* She was obviously not going to tell him her husband's name right now.

"I'll be right back."

He was up on deck, handing a wad of pesos to the supplier, when certain things began to register.

The woman lying in his bed had chestnut brown hair. He hadn't noticed until she turned away from him and he got a good look at her ponytail. Even then, the rich reddish brown color hadn't really sunk in until he'd looked back at her once more before walking out of the cabin.

Other things started filtering into his brain as well. Her calves were extremely well toned, like those of a dancer . . . or a showgirl. She'd spit out *Colton Denning* with a lot of contempt, but also as if answering his question, which implied something totally impossible.

That he was her husband.

Fayre lay on the bed and willed her stomach to settle and her tears to cease. She'd done all the crying over Colton Denning she was going to do. Wasn't that what she'd promised herself? Hadn't she come to make him face up to his responsibilities, not grieve the sorry bastard's lack of a conscience.

But how could he act like he didn't even know her?

As if they'd never even met. As if he'd never sweet talked her into believing it *had* been love at first sight for him. That he wanted to marry her more than he wanted anything else in life. *Come on, girl. He walked out on you, turning your so-called marriage into a one-night stand.*

Her stomach cramped, and she willed herself to calm down.

"*Are you trying to say you are my wife?*"

She flipped onto her back in shock at the volume of the words that reverberated in the small room.

Pushing herself up into a sitting position, she was grateful her stomach didn't start heaving again. "Are you trying to say you don't remember?"

"I don't."

"Right. You've got amnesia." She might look like a bimbo, but she wasn't one.

She believed that fairy tale like she believed Cinderella had been a historical figure. Not.

The bulging muscles of his big body went tense, and sexy lips that had done incredible things to her body at one time thinned into a frown. He brushed his hand over his head, almost as if running his fingers through the nonexistent black hair he'd had shaved close to his head.

Then his dark brown eyes bore into her with intense concentration. "Why don't we start by you telling me why you're claiming to be my wife."

Chapter Three

"I don't believe you."

This man could not be for real. He'd been all over her, calling her angel. This *honey* thing was a new one. So was the way he held himself so stiff and did the whole silent-man routine. The man she'd met six weeks ago had been fun loving, funny and so sexy she'd melted at his touch.

The touch thing was still iffy. It had felt way too good when he held her, making her believe she was safe in his arms. Just like he had in Vegas, but it was a lie. He was trying to pretend he didn't even remember meeting her.

No safety there. No protection. Just pain.

"I'm claiming to be your wife because I am." She barely suppressed tagging on a *you jerk*.

She was going to be grown up about this thing. He'd hurt her, but she'd been the idiot who believed him in the first place. She knew she didn't deserve the kind of pain she was in right now, but she couldn't help feeling it was inevitable when linked with that kind of stupidity.

His big hands clenched and unclenched. "Do you have some proof of your claim?"

"Stop it." She couldn't stand this anymore. "Stop playing this game with me. It's not fair."

"I'm not playing a game." He sounded angry, but his eyes were way too gentle for the tenor of his voice. "I need to know when I was supposed to have married you."

She named their wedding date, and he closed those gorgeous brown eyes, leaning back against the wall of the cabin, his dark skin taking on a gray cast. "You're the woman who was in my bed in Vegas."

The words slapped her with their impersonal implications. He hadn't even given her a name. She was just the woman he'd had sex with in Vegas.

He looked like such a decent guy. How could he demean her like that? And they'd done more than have sex. They'd gotten married, and he could damn well admit it.

"I did more than screw you. I married you, and contrary to what you obviously think, quicky Vegas weddings *are* legally binding."

"I don't doubt the legality of our supposed marriage, but I don't remember it either."

"It isn't a supposed marriage. It's a real marriage. On paper anyway and I've got the marriage certificate to prove it." Not that she wanted to stay married to this jerk.

She'd heard Mexican divorces were as quick as Vegas weddings. Tomorrow, she had every intention of finding out.

Coming after him had been one more stupid thing to do in a long line of them. She should have waited for him to come back to the States and just served him divorce papers, but she'd gone a little nuts, her rational thought processes going on hiatus. She could blame it on her hormones.

All of which left her in a tiny town in rural Mexico, trying to make a man who had no intention of even acknowledging their wedding stand up to his responsibilities.

Not going to happen.

"I'd like to see it."

She swung her feet off the side of the bed and stood up.

Still a little woozy, she moved slowly. "I'll show it to you tomorrow when we file for divorce."

She had no idea if Las Playas del Blanco had a courthouse, but Puerto Vallarta was just a few hours south.

She started walking through the door, but his hand snaked out so fast she didn't even see it until his fingers were wrapped in a loose hold around her bicep.

"Where are you going?"

"To find a motel. You can meet me at the taverna tomorrow morning, and we'll deal with the divorce then."

"The only motel in Las Playas del Blanco is above the taverna. You can't stay there."

She tilted her head to look at him. It hurt, but she made herself keep eye contact. "Why not? Is it full, or something?"

"You saw what the taverna is like. Garcia will be there tonight, looking for a way to restore his machismo. He might decide banging down your door just might be the way to do it."

"Then I'll drive out of town and sleep in my car somewhere. Whatever. What I do has nothing to do with you."

"You said that I'm your husband."

"And you're denying it." Was this guy nuts, or was she? Suddenly tired of arguing, she yanked her arm from his grasp. "I'll stay where I darn well please."

"You're being hasty. We have a lot to discuss, and there's no reason for you to take off." The soothing tone of his voice was at odds with the tense stance of his body.

"There's every reason. I don't know what weird game you're playing, but I'm not going there."

"Honey—"

"No." She put her hand up, completely incapable of dealing with that one small endearment. "You've made your position very clear. I was a one-night stand that got out of hand. The marriage meant nothing to you and neither do I. Fine.

I've got it. We'll file for divorce tomorrow, then go our separate ways as if we'd never met."

Well, okay, she wouldn't be able to act as if she'd never met him, but she was getting out of his life, and then she was going to do something about picking up the pieces of her own.

His hand clamped down on her shoulder, this time the hold a whole lot firmer than it had been before. "I don't remember that night. I'm not trying to blow you off."

She rolled her eyes. Right. "I want to leave now."

His jaw went rigid, as though he was trying to hold something in. "No."

"*No?* Look, buddy—"

"I was drunk, all right? I never drink, and I consumed an entire bottle of champagne. I do not remember anything after the third glass."

She stared at him.

Truth burned down at her from his dark brown eyes.

No, she'd believed those eyes once. This time he wasn't fooling her. "You were drunk my fanny. You were sober enough to talk me into a wedding night. Like hell you were sauced."

She turned to leave, pulling away from him, but found herself swept up into his arms for the second time that day. She immediately tried to get loose, but his hold was too firm. Not painfully tight, but impossible to break.

He carried her to the armchair and sat down with her in his lap. She tried to get up, but the only change she affected was under her left hip.

He was getting a hard-on.

She hit his chest with her fist. "No. Don't you even think you're going there. I'm never letting you touch me again."

"*I'm sorry.* I can't help it. Stop squirming and maybe I can recite multiplication tables or something until it goes away." He sounded really irritated, and she glared at him.

But she stopped moving.

He sighed, like he was really relieved.

"If you hadn't picked me up like some big ape and set me down in your lap, neither of us would be uncomfortable."

"You were set on leaving, and we need to talk."

"All we need is to file for a quick Mexican divorce, and then we can both put this whole sorry mess behind us."

"That is not going to happen."

She remembered when he'd said that in the bar. He'd used the same mean tone, and she wasn't drunk like that idiot who'd tried to manhandle her. She was sober enough to realize Colton meant business.

"What exactly do you want to talk about?" Maybe if he said whatever it was he needed to say, he'd let her go, and she could find a nice private place to fall apart.

"Tell me what happened that night."

She opened her mouth to blast him again, and he must have known it because his big hand gently covered her lips, effectively cutting her off.

"When I'm drunk, I act like I'm sober, except I'm a lot friendlier. If you need verification, I'll let you call my mother. Moonbeam will tell you that I'm not a fall-down drunk, just a goofy one."

Moonbeam? This guy had a mother named Moonbeam? She could have believed that of the man she met six weeks ago, but not Mr. Sobersides.

"You didn't act goofy," she mumbled against his hand.

He moved it. "What?"

"You didn't act goofy."

"I talked you into marrying me the same night we met. In my book, that's goofy behavior."

Colton wanted to cut out his own tongue as he watched her face tighten with pain and lose color once again. Damn it, he'd hurt her, and he hadn't meant to. He'd been trying to explain, but he realized his explanations were not going to go over well with her.

204 / Lucy Monroe

"You weren't drunk that night, were you?"

She shook her head, vulnerability shining in her green eyes and reaching out to wrap around his heart.

He'd been out of his mind, but she hadn't been. That meant that when she agreed to marry him, she'd wanted it. As improbable as it might seem, she had really wanted him. His leaving her, forgetting her, denying their marriage . . . they'd all hurt her. A lot.

He wished he could believe something else.

Like that she was an opportunist who had taken advantage of him, a woman who had realized he was a rich man and had engineered the wedding with an eye toward a hefty divorce settlement. That picture of her didn't ring true, however.

For two reasons.

The first was that he knew he did not act drunk, which meant she'd had no way of knowing that he wasn't operating under his normal superconservative approach to life.

The second was, she was too damn defenseless.

He was a pretty good judge of character when he wasn't drunk, and his gut was telling him that this woman had married him in good faith. Which meant what? That she'd believed herself in love?

From the lethal expression in her green gaze, he figured she was no longer under any such illusion.

"I'm sorry." He didn't know what else to say.

Nothing he said would undo the damage he'd done to her already.

"Me, too." She turned her head, but he could see the tears leaking out of her eyes, and this time he knew their cause.

Him.

It was like taking a punch to the gut without tightening his muscles first.

He pulled her to his chest and wrapped his arms around

her. "Shh . . . It's going to be okay. We're going to work this out."

She shook her head and pushed against him, but when he held tight the fight drained out of her, and she let him cuddle her. "How can it be okay?" The words were muffled by his chest, but he heard them. "You don't even know my name."

He'd known six weeks ago that would be a problem, and now it seemed like a mountain he had no way of climbing over.

"What is it?"

"Fayre Denning." She sucked in a huge breath and then let it out. "I mean Cranston. I'm not really a Denning."

Aw, crap. He couldn't stand the sadness in her voice.

"Fayre's a beautiful name."

"Thanks. You thought the same thing the night we met."

He lifted her face away from his chest, his hand under her chin. She'd stopped crying, but her eyes were empty of emotion, and he didn't like that any better. "Will you tell me about it? Please."

She sighed and nodded. "But could I have some water first, and maybe some soda crackers?"

How could he have forgotten her nausea? "Sure, honey." He stood up with her still tucked in his arms and started heading toward the galley.

"You don't have to carry me."

"I like it."

She hit him again, and it shocked him into stopping.

"What was that for?"

"Don't say stuff like that. You don't mean it."

He'd hurt her, all right, and he didn't know if he could undo the damage, but he had to try.

Because holding her didn't just feel good, it felt right, and he wasn't letting her go for a quick Mexican divorce before they explored the possibilities of their unexpected marriage.

Chapter Four

Fayre tried not to slump into the bench at the small table in the galley.

She was not a slumping sort of person. She was a glass half-full type of woman. Life had never gotten her down for long, no matter how hard it was, and growing up in the foster care system had thrown a few stones her way. But this gig was doing things to her heart that were really challenging her positive attitude.

Like obliterating it.

He really did not remember her. At all.

How demoralizing was that?

Colton set a glass of water in front of her and a small plate of crackers. "Is this all right?"

She nodded and picked up the glass of water. Beyond thirsty, she drank half of it before setting it down again. Then she started nibbling on a cracker.

Colton sat down across from her, a quiet brooding presence.

"I'm a dancer in the follies." She didn't know why she started with that bit of information. It wasn't exactly the most important piece of news she had to impart, but it just popped out.

"I figured that much out the morning after."

Thinking of the morning after was not good for her emotional well-being, so she ignored his comment. "You came backstage after our last show and you . . . I don't know how to put this without sounding like a total bimbo."

"I won't think you're a bimbo, no matter what you say, okay?"

He seemed really serious about that, so she nodded.

"You swept me off my feet. Literally. You picked me up and told me you'd fallen in love at first sight. You'd paid to watch the second show just so you could watch me, you said." Embarrassment crawled up her skin. "I fell for it like a mentally challenged ton of bricks."

It had felt so right in his arms, and something *had* happened to *her* heart the first time she looked into his warm and, she could have sworn, *loving* brown eyes.

"I must have been very persuasive."

"You were." He'd been so horny and such a gentleman at the same time, careful not to overwhelm her physically, but he'd let her know he wanted her from the first moment. The fact he didn't try to cop a feel had been one of the reasons she'd gone to eat with him. "You took me to supper. We talked for something like three hours."

He looked appalled. "About what?"

Now that she thought about it, he probably didn't want to know how much of his private life he'd shared with a complete stranger. She'd never been good at lying, so she told him, but hoped to keep it vague. It would be less disturbing for both of them.

"Your family. My family." Or lack thereof. "You told me about the brothers you'd just met and how the three of you were coming down here to look for lithium deposits on Luna Island."

The look of horror was growing.

"Don't worry. I didn't take an ad out in the *Vegas Times* or anything. Okay?"

"Did I tell you about Moonbeam?"

"She's your mom, right? You had a lot to say about her, but you didn't tell me her name."

He'd talked about what it had been like growing up the son of a flower child from the sixties who had never really grown up herself. How hard it had been to have a dad who had given only one concession to his existence—financial support. Moonbeam's lifestyle choices had made Colton uncomfortable. The taciturn nature of the man before her made a lot more sense when Fayre considered the things he'd said that night, than the man who had so effectively seduced her body and heart.

"And you told me about your family?"

"Yes." He'd forgotten, and she wasn't about to elaborate now. It wasn't the same, and she saw no reason to expose her past to a man she planned to divorce the next day.

"You said we talked for three hours?"

"Yes." She had felt as if she knew him better than friends she'd had since coming to Vegas when she was eighteen and full of crazy dreams. "Then you asked me to marry you. I thought you were insane, but you were adamant. You talked me into it, and we got married." It was an extremely simplified version of how he'd begged her to marry him, had promised to love her forever and give her the family she'd never had. "Then we went back to your hotel room and made lo . . . had sex."

His gorgeous face was set in unemotional lines that worried her. "We used a lot of condoms for the few hours we could have spent in bed."

Typical of a man to notice that kind of thing.

"We broke two of them. You were pretty impatient."

He was back to looking horrified. "Did I force you?"

She rolled her eyes and munched on a cracker before answering. "Don't be a dolt. Do you really think I would have come all the way down here after you if you'd treated me badly in bed? Trust me, if you'd *tried* to force me, I would not be sitting here and neither would you."

"I left without saying goodbye." He said it like that was just as bad.

And it was. It had hurt more than she would ever admit to him. If she hadn't had other reasons for coming after him, she probably never would have.

"You left a note." The words were indelibly imprinted on her memory.

Thanks for everything. The room is paid through tomorrow, so you don't have to rush getting out of here. He'd signed it with a *C*. Not even his full name.

"I'm sorry," he said again.

It didn't help any more this time than it had before. She was sorry, too, but they had embarked on a path that she had no choice but to follow to completion.

She shrugged, wondering how to tell him the rest of it.

"The last thing I remember was watching you dance. You looked like an angel."

"So that was why."

He took a drink. "Why what?"

"You kept calling me angel instead of Fayre. The next day, after I woke up alone, I figured it was the name you used for all your women."

"I don't have a lot of women. I'm not a player."

"You could have fooled me."

"I wasn't myself that night, Fayre."

"So you've said." And, damn it, she believed him.

Which left her in a really bad place.

He'd been drunk, not himself, and the consequences of that night weren't going to sit well on him. She just knew it. She'd suspected before coming down to Mexico, but then she'd believed he deserved to have his life disrupted like hers was. She wasn't feeling all that self-righteous now.

Just dumbfounded and a little scared.

"Anyway, I called you angel because that's what you looked like to me with that big feather headdress and the white shimmery cape you used in your final number."

She stared at him, feeling the nausea returning. "You just described the outfit for the lead dancer in our show. I danced in the chorus."

She couldn't believe it. Not only had he not really had any feelings for her, but the lust at first sight he'd experienced had been for their show's lead, Candy.

It just figured.

"I . . ." He was at a loss for words, and she could understand why.

It was all such a mess.

"You must have come backstage looking for Candy and found me instead." What were the chances? "There's something funny in that; give me a minute and I'll find it."

The hitch in Fayre's voice told Colton that she saw nothing humorous at all in the fact he'd believed her to be the angel he watched dancing onstage.

"You're the one I spent three hours talking to."

She looked at him like he'd lost his mind. "I'm the one you forgot. You remember Candy, who you never even spoke to, and you forgot me, the woman you married and had sex with. I'm supposed to feel better because we had a conversation you have no recollection of? Give me a break."

"I told you, I don't remember anything after the third glass of champagne." His subconscious did, though, and the dreams were enough to send him over the deep end without a paddle.

She snorted, her sensual mouth pursing. "You didn't have to remember anything to see me in your bed the next morning. And you still left without a word. I guess I was pretty unmemorable sober as well, wasn't I?"

212 / *Lucy Monroe*

He wanted to look away. Those green eyes were filled with accusation and a pain he couldn't deal with, but he forced himself to focus on her dead on.

"I woke up with the daddy of all hangovers and in bed with a stranger. Your face was hidden by your hair. I couldn't remember anything, and I was kicking my own ass mentally for having unprotected sex with a woman I'd never met before."

"We used condoms."

He rubbed his hand over his face. "Yeah. I was pretty relieved when I realized that. And I figured I owed you for taking the precautions because I'm pretty sure I didn't think of it."

"You didn't."

"Thank you for taking care of it."

She averted her face, and her bottom lip began to tremble. She bit it.

"What is it?"

Something really serious was bothering her, more than just him forgetting who she was. He could feel it. He didn't know how or why, but he was definitely in tune with this woman.

"We didn't use a condom the last time."

"Why the hell not?" Wrong thing to say.

He knew it the minute the words were out of his mouth, but by then it was too late.

Green eyes fried him with furious flames. "You want to know why we didn't use a glove the last time we made love?"

At least she wasn't calling it having sex again. That bugged him, and he didn't care why.

She leaned across the table. "You, Mr. Persuasive, wanted to make love again, but we'd used the last condom. You told me you were clean, and I knew I was. You touched me until I was dying with pleasure and then said, 'Don't worry about it, Fayre. Would it really be that bad to start a family right away? Let's make a baby, angel.' And I bought it."

Unease crawled up his insides.

He looked at the soda crackers she'd been steadily nibbling throughout their conversation. She didn't have Montezuma's Revenge, or a stomach bug.

"We made a baby, didn't we? That's why you tracked me down here."

She didn't say anything, but her expression said it all.

"Hell."

She erupted out of her seat and glared at him. "Don't worry about it, Mr. Denning. I don't expect anything from you. I was the idiot who believed in the fairy tale, and I'll be the one to deal with the consequences."

She went to sweep by him, but he stopped her. Again. She had a real thing for trying to leave before they were done talking. He supposed he couldn't blame her after the way he'd left her, but she couldn't drop a bomb like that and just leave.

They had to deal with the aftermath. "Wait."

"No. Tomorrow we file for divorce, and then you can forget you ever met me. *It shouldn't be too hard.*"

He winced at the dig, but he didn't let her go. "I'm not going to forget you're pregnant with my baby."

"It's nothing to do with you."

"How can you say that? I'm your baby's father."

"You're nothing in my life, Mr. Denning. Nothing." She spat the words out with a passion that singed him.

"You don't plan to have the baby?"

Had she come all the way down here to ask him to pay for an abortion?

If her glare had been hot before, now it was sulfuric. "I'm not killing my baby for your convenience."

"I didn't ask you to." Just the thought made him sick.

"You just said—"

"You said I was nothing in your life. I thought that meant you planned to get rid of the baby."

"Your communication skills need a lot of work."

"Moonbeam says the same thing." He tried for a small smile, but Fayre stood in stone-faced silence, not responding at all. "Look, you can't leave right now."

"I can, and what's more, that's exactly what I'm going to do. I'll drive down to Puerto Vallarta tonight. You can meet me there tomorrow, and we'll file the paperwork."

Las Playas del Blanco had a courthouse of sorts, but he wasn't about to tell her that. They were filing for divorce over his dead body. "You can't drive all the way to Puerto Vallarta alone."

"Why not? I drove all the way here from Vegas by myself."

He didn't know what he'd thought—that she'd flown into Puerto Vallarta and taken the bus up maybe. Which was bad enough, but he'd never even considered that she'd driven all the way from Vegas on her own. "You're a woman."

"So?"

"That was a totally stupid thing to do. You could have been hurt, mugged, stopped along the way by men with ugly intentions. Anything could have happened to you."

Her little chin set at a stubborn angle, and he had a totally inappropriate-to-the-circumstances urge to kiss that luscious pink mouth until she was moaning with need.

"Nothing happened to me."

"Well, if you think I'm going to let you go traipsing off to Puerto Vallarta, you're straight-on crazy."

Her eyes widened with more surprise than anger. *"Like you have anything to say about it."*

"I have plenty."

"How do you figure that?" Belligerent, she was pretty damn enticing.

It gave him an atavistic urge to tame her fire. He wondered how he could have remembered any woman but this one. She was so hot, his insides burned just looking at her.

"I'm your husband," he reminded her with exasperation.

"Not too long ago you were asking for proof of that."

"Well, I don't need it now."

"Why not?"

What was it with women? She'd been deeply offended by his doubt in the first place, and now she was acting equally offended that he didn't need to see the certificate to believe they were married.

"You're only my husband on paper, and that will change tomorrow." Her eyes glittered with challenge, and her entire body defied him.

He towered over her, so frustrated he was ready to explode. "Like hell that's going to change."

Chapter Five

"Are you saying you want to stay married?"

Not in all the fantasies she'd had about her meeting up with Colton again had she entertained the concept he might want to stay married. In her mind, he'd made his contempt of the marriage clear when he'd disappeared the next morning without a word. Finding out he didn't remember any of it didn't change the initial premise—that she meant nothing to him.

It couldn't. Not after finding out she wasn't even the woman he'd intended to seduce that night.

She wasn't his angel.

"Yes." His intensity was a little frightening, and she wanted to step back, creating some distance between them, but he still had a hold on her arms. "I definitely plan on us staying married."

"That's ridiculous."

"You're pregnant with my baby." One of his hands dropped to settle over her lower abdomen in a possessive gesture that scared her because it felt so right. "I talked you into getting this way. Staying married doesn't seem ridiculous to me. It seems like the right thing to do."

She'd been listening with rapt attention right up until he

said it was *the right thing to do*. Was she ever, just once in her life, going to be somebody's best choice instead of an obligation they felt they had to fulfill?

Okay, so she admired him for wanting to do the honorable thing, but couldn't he care about *her*, just a little? She couldn't live with a marriage motivated by his overdeveloped sense of honor.

"You can't build a marriage on guilt and a night of great sex." Especially one he couldn't even recall. "It takes more than that to merge two people's lives."

"According to you, it will be three people pretty soon." His hand caressed her tummy. "Six weeks ago, you believed our lives could merge just fine."

"I was . . ." She tossed around in her mind for an excuse for her unbelievably naive behavior.

He shook his head. "You already said you weren't drunk when you agreed to marry me; that means you meant it."

The reminder that she'd been the sober idiot while he'd been the drunk one snapped what was left of her emotional control. Using a move she'd learned in self-defense class, she broke his hold and sent the huge man tumbling to the galley floor.

It wouldn't have worked if he'd been willing to hurt her to keep her with him, but she'd known he wasn't and taken shameless advantage of it. Unwilling to wait around for him to decide how to deal with her again, she jumped over his long legs and rushed up the stairs to the boat's deck.

Seconds later, she vaulted onto the dock from the gangplank. Sprinting as if she were competing in the Olympic hundred-yard dash, she headed for her car. She'd left it parked near the taverna, which wasn't far from the dock.

If she was lucky, she'd reach it before he could catch up with her . . . if he chased after her at all.

"Fayre!"

Oh, he was chasing all right. She looked back over her

shoulder and bit back a scream. He was gaining on her, and the look in his eyes was anything but tame.

She turned her attention back to the ground in front of her and tried to run faster. Her breath was already billowing in and out, and she could feel sweat slithering down her back and temples. Increasing her pace made it worse, but she didn't care. She had to get away from him.

She reached her little Beetle with a sense of relief that lasted as long as it took her to dig the key out of her pocket and get it into the lock on the driver's side door. Two huge hands landed on either side of her, blocking her from opening the car. Colton's overmuscled body pressed against her back, hemming her in as effectively as if she'd stepped into a closet made of bricks.

His breath wasn't nearly as labored as hers, and for that alone she wanted to kick him.

"What's the matter with you, Fayre?" He didn't shout, but she had no doubt about the level of his displeasure. The man was pissed. "You can't go running like that when you're pregnant. What if you'd tripped and fallen?"

"I'm stupid about men, not clumsy. I'm a dancer, remember?" Maybe she hadn't been his angel and the lead of the show, but Fayre could at least lay claim to graceful in her self-description.

Landing a job as a dancer in even the chorus of the follies was not something to scoff at.

"Yeah, well, you're also my wife." His voice rumbled next to her ear, sending shivers of awareness down to her toes. "You aren't going haring off anywhere in this little excuse for a car."

That was it!

She spun to face him and poked his chest with her forefinger. "You take that back. My car is wonderful!"

"Your car is a lime green toy only marginally larger than my bathtub." He wasn't looking at the car, however. He was looking at her, and from the expression on his face, her sweaty, bedraggled appearance didn't bother him one iota.

His eyes were locked on her lips.

"It must be a big bathtub because my car is not a toy." How could he disparage Esmerelda that way? That little car was her pride and joy. She'd saved like a miser so she could buy one of the very first new VW Beetles when they were released.

"It is." And still his gaze did not waver from her lips. "I'm a big man."

"I noticed."

He was big all over.

Crowding her closer to the car, his brown gaze went dark with a reaction she'd gotten to know very well six weeks ago. Passionate desire. He wanted her, and if the feral look in his eyes hadn't given him away, the huge hard-on pressing against her stomach would have.

She couldn't go this route again. *"No."*

"I need to kiss you, Fayre."

"I—"

He cut her off with his lips.

Lips that she knew, a mouth she remembered, a kiss she'd craved throughout the hours of their wedding night and every darn day since.

He kissed her as though his mouth remembered her, even if his mind didn't. He knew exactly how much pressure she liked, how to get her lips to part for his tongue, how to coax a response even when she didn't want to give one.

Her hands slid up his chest of their own volition, not stopping until they were locked behind his neck. She didn't have to push her body into his because he was doing it for her. Pressing her into the heated metal of her car door, his equally hot body molded every inch of her front.

And the kiss turned carnal, two hungry mouths attempting to devour each other under the hot Mexican sun.

He tasted good, even better than she remembered. His body was so hard, so big and so strong. She knew intimately how much pleasure her body was capable of experiencing with it, and the knowledge did as much to heat her insides as the feel of his mouth rocking over hers.

His pelvis thrust toward her, making both of them moan.

Remembered pleasure arced through her body as he touched her in ways that had haunted her dreams and left her sleep broken with unsatisfied longings.

His hands came down and cupped her buttocks, pulling her body up until their pelvises matched. She spread her legs and locked them around his hips, increasing the pressure of his hardness against the place that needed it most.

Groaning, he broke his mouth away from hers and kissed her face, her eyelids, the sensitive spot below her ear. He licked it, and she arched her neck, wanting more. His body continued to move against hers as if he was making love to her with their clothes on. Pretty soon, she was going to climax.

He nuzzled into her neck. "Angel, you smell so good."

Fayre erupted like a Fury who had found the mythological Orestes, shoving at Colton, trying to get away, and she felt every bit as volatile as those three beings were supposed to have been.

"I'm not . . ." She unwrapped her legs from around him and tried to push him away at the same time. "Your angel. That's Candy, *remember?*"

How could she have been so stupid? Again?

She'd been seconds away from letting him make love to her again, and she wasn't even *his* angel!

"*Let me go.*" She couldn't stand having him touch her and knowing it was another woman he'd wanted that night.

He wasn't listening. His lips were still wreaking havoc on her neck, and his big hands kneaded her backside with a lot more skill than a man who professed to be so conservative with women should have.

She tried to grab his hair, to hold his head away, but there was nothing to take hold of in the black hair cropped so close to his head. Feeling desperate, she shoved her hand in front of his mouth, preventing him from kissing her again.

His lips were hot, and his tongue flicked out to caress her palm.

It took every bit of her resolve to stick with her decision to cut off the kiss. "Knock it off, Colton. I'm not making this mistake with you again."

His head came up, his expression dazed, his lips still pressed against her sensitive palm.

He mumbled something into her tingling flesh that she didn't understand, so she warily let her hand drop. He didn't try to kiss her again, but he looked as though he wanted to.

"It wasn't a mistake."

Maybe not for him. "Oh, yes, it was, and I'm not repeating it. I should never have trusted you in the first place."

He reared back, looking offended.

Finally free of his hold, she sagged against the car, not completely over the effects of his seduction techniques.

"You can trust me."

"That's why you left me without a word. Get a grip, Colton. You're just another bad choice in men for me in a long line of them. If I were nearly as smart as I want to be, I would run for cover the minute I think I can trust a man, because that's a sure sign I can't."

"If I'd been in my right mind, I would never have left you."

"If you'd been in your right mind, you would have taken Candy to supper, not me, and none of this would have happened."

Or maybe it would have, only with Candy playing center stage just like she did in the follies and Fayre fading into the background. The idea made her stomach cramp again, and she glared at him.

"But I didn't take that other woman. I took you, and now we're married. You can trust me from here on out, Fayre. I'm not the type of man who dumps on women."

She remembered him saying something very similar on the night they met. "Because you figure your dad dumped on your mom and you were the result."

His jaw went taut, but he didn't answer.

She didn't need him to. He'd told her all about it the night they got married.

"Your perception of dumping and mine must be really different, because *you are* the guy who walked out without a word and left me naked and alone in bed."

He rubbed his hand over his head in what she'd come to realize was his gesture denoting frustration. "I've regretted doing so ever since."

"That's so easy to say now."

"It's true, damn it." His big body vibrated with intensity. "I wanted to call, to apologize, but I couldn't remember your name."

"Like that's supposed to make me feel better?"

He glowered at her. "I planned to come back to Vegas and find you. I wanted to apologize."

"Right." But could it be true? She so desperately wanted it to be true, but then she gave herself a mental kick. What difference would an apology have made? He wasn't saying he had planned to come back and try to establish a relationship or something. "I don't need your remorse."

"But I am sorry, honey. I'm sorry I left you still sleeping in my bed. I'm sorry I can't remember anything. I'm s—"

"Apology accepted. Now will you just let me leave?" She couldn't stand one more *sorry.*

He shook his head. "You're not being rational right now, Fayre."

"I'm being perfectly sensible. We both made a mistake,

and the most *rational* thing to do now is to rectify that mistake. Which we'll do tomorrow at the Puerto Vallarta courthouse."

His hand snaked out, and before she realized what was happening, he'd unlocked her car door, popped her trunk, gone around to it and bent down to rummage inside. When he stood up, he had her suitcase, her makeup bag and other sundry items belonging to her.

"What do you think you are doing?"

"We need to talk."

She rolled her eyes. "Stealing my suitcase isn't going to make me talk to you."

"Isn't it?"

He banged the trunk shut, closed her car door and put the keys in his pocket.

She crossed her arms over her chest. "Do you really think you can blackmail me into talking to you?"

He didn't even bother to answer. He just started walking back to the boat. He'd turned the corner around the taverna before she let it sink in that he really had no intention of even discussing his incredibly *irrational* behavior.

She realized something else at the same time. Without her car keys and the stuff Colton had confiscated from her trunk, she couldn't go anywhere. She barely had enough money in her pocket to buy herself dinner; she definitely didn't have enough to get one of those rooms above the taverna.

Of course, she could always tell them to bill Colton.

Only the thought of going back into that smoke-filled room made her nauseous, and she really didn't want another run-in with the local male population.

But she'd be darned if she was going to tamely follow Colton to his boat like a pet dog or something.

If he could be stubborn, so could she.

She sat down in the dirt on the side of the car that was in the shade. It wasn't the side facing the road that led around the taverna, but she had no intention of watching for him like some lovesick teenager anyway.

He'd figure out soon enough that his little game wasn't going to work, and he'd come back.

She'd just have to wait him out.

Twenty minutes later, she smiled to herself when a shadow longer than her car fell over her. It hadn't taken him very long to figure out she wasn't budging. She schooled her features into an unemotional mask before looking up. He wasn't the type of man that would respond well to gloating when he was beaten and might feel the need to prove himself.

She didn't get a chance to say anything gloating or otherwise because he bent over and picked her up just like he had when she'd suffered morning sickness in the bar.

And darned if she didn't feel just as safe as she had then.

It was an illusion. She knew it was, but still, the feeling persisted.

"What do you think you are doing?"

"Kidnapping you."

Chapter Six

He said it so calmly that she didn't get the meaning of his words right off. When she did, she about choked on her own breath.

"What do you mean? Kidnapping me? You can't do that."

"I'm doing it." He said it with irritating complacence.

"You can't." Okay, maybe he could, since he was carrying her toward his boat without the least difficulty. But he couldn't get away with it. "I'll go to the police. I'll press charges."

He looked down at her, and it was only then that she realized he wasn't nearly as calm as he was putting on. "We're in rural Mexico, Fayre. You're my wife, no matter how you want to look at it. As far as the local police are concerned, this wouldn't even rate typing up the complaint. They'd laugh you right out of their office."

She said something really foul, and he smiled a not very nice smile.

"Exactly. Accept it. *We are going to talk*. We are not going to file for divorce tomorrow, and you *are* going to take a lot better care of yourself than you've been doing."

"Kidnapping is not taking care of me." She couldn't believe she had to point that out.

"It is when you're intent on being self-destructive."

228 / Lucy Monroe

"Self-destructive was marrying you. Divorce is me waking up and finally getting a little self-protective."

"Are all pregnant women this illogical?"

"I am not illogical."

"You are when you try to imply that divorcing the father of your child before you even discuss options is the smart thing to do. It's not."

"You are not my husband!" He couldn't remember the marriage, therefore it was null and void in her mind.

"I have a marriage certificate that says I am."

"You have . . ."

"It was in your trunk, sitting on top of some other papers. I grabbed it along with your passport and money."

"Larceny is a crime."

"What's mine is yours, baby, and vice versa. I can't steal from you because you're my wife."

"So, you're saying if I went down to the bank and withdrew all the money in your checking account, that wouldn't be stealing?"

"As soon as we get this little issue of divorce worked out, I'll take you to the bank myself and put you on my account."

"You're crazy." No way was he going to put a virtual stranger on his accounts. He owned his own mining company. "You're rich, for goodness' sake. I could drain your accounts and take off."

"You won't." He said it with such authority she called him crazy again.

"No, crazy was leaving you alone in that bed and running away like a scared adolescent."

They had reached the boat, and he carried her on board. "Do you want to sit in the pilot house with me, or would you rather rest in the cabin?"

"You're not listening to anything I say," she accused.

"I'll listen if you tell me which you'd prefer. I promise."

"I don't want to be on this boat at all."

"Don't worry. The ride to Luna Island isn't that long. Are you worried you'll get sick again?"

"If I do, I'm going to throw up on your shoe."

He looked singularly unworried by that threat. "Then I'll have to hope you don't get sick, won't I?"

His scent was getting to her, so was that tone of voice. It wasn't just reasonable. It was indulgent. He talked to her and looked at her as though she was something, someone . . . to be cherished.

"I know it's all a ruse, so don't think you're going to fool me."

"What, angel?"

She stiffened at the endearment, but since he was neither drunk, nor under the influence of overwhelming passion, she couldn't accuse him of not knowing what he was saying.

"You don't care about *me*. I'm just a duty to you, me and my baby."

His smile was even more indulgent and tender than his voice had been. "You're too beautiful and sexy to be a mere duty to anyone."

She harrumphed, and he kissed the tip of her nose.

"It's true, and believe me when I tell you, I'll never look at our child as anything but *our child*. Not a duty, not an embarrassment and never a mistake."

His expression had turned serious again, his eyes boring a message into her that she was terrified of believing.

She'd been let down too many times in the past.

Most recently by this very man.

She had to remember that, but it was getting harder and harder to concentrate on how he'd hurt her.

He seemed so intent on fixing it.

Colton carried Fayre's things to the house he'd been using as a base while excavating for lithium on Luna Island.

It was far enough away from the rest of his employees and

their operation to afford some privacy, but it wasn't so far that Fayre couldn't make the trip easily walking.

Not that she would have balked at climbing a mountain or anything. The woman had no concept of what it meant to be in a *delicate* condition. As feminine and sweet as she was, she did not see herself as delicate in any way. *Incredible.* She had this amazing belief she could handle anything.

Which had resulted in her driving all the way to rural Mexico from Vegas by herself. He got chills every time he let himself think of everything that could have happened to her on that drive. He could only thank God none of it had.

They climbed the steps to the porch and walked inside the cool interior of the house; all the while their silence remained unbroken. Fayre hadn't said much on the boat ride over either. She'd pretty much sat there, looking out over the water, her expression pensive, her posture tense.

Not that he could blame her for being tense. He'd kidnapped her, for heaven's sake.

What had he been thinking?

That he didn't want her driving to Puerto Vallarta and filing for a divorce, that's what.

So, he'd committed the most irrational act of his life and kidnapped a woman.

He stopped in the doorway to one of the guest bedrooms his brothers used when they came to confer with him over findings. "You can sleep in here."

"Is this your room?" For such a sweet woman, she sure could sound mean.

"No." He gestured down the hall with his head. "I'm down there. Second door on your right."

"If your sister-in-law never lived here, how did this house get built?"

So he'd told her about the island belonging to Phoebe? He wondered what else he'd told Fayre. It had been enough for her to believe she knew him sufficiently well to marry him. It had been enough to make her trust him.

She sure as hell did not trust him now, and it was his own damn fault.

He'd walked out on her the morning after, and even if he hadn't remembered their marriage, he'd known they'd gone to bed together.

"Colton?"

He realized he'd never answered her question, but stood there like a simpleton in the doorway of her temporary room. "Phoebe's great uncle liked to vacation here. He had the house built a couple of decades ago. It doesn't have air-conditioning, but the high ceilings and fans in every room keep things pretty cool."

"It's surrounded by trees. Do any of the rooms get direct sunlight?"

"No." It had taken some getting used to at first, but he'd come to appreciate that idiosyncrasy in architecture pretty quickly as the temperatures rose.

She sidled past him into the room and stopped to look around. "It's like the inside of a California mission."

He looked at the simple furniture, the whitewashed adobe walls, and had to agree. "Will you be all right in here?"

Her gaze shifted to the doorway to her private bathroom, and she nodded. "I'll be fine."

"Are you still mad?"

The words had just slipped out. Stupid question. Of course she was still angry. Twentieth-century women did not take to being kidnapped.

She shrugged, her movement almost defensive when she had nothing to be defensive about. He was the one who'd done the reprehensible. Even knowing that, he'd do it again rather than let her climb into her little green car and drive out of his life.

"I was being irrational." She sighed, sounding tired. "We do need to talk. I'm not saying I appreciate the strong-arm tactics, but I'm not going to hold a grudge."

He reached out and brushed her cheek. Her skin was so soft. "You're an amazing woman."

She went completely still, her attention fixed wholly on him.

He let his hand slide down to cup her shoulder. It was getting harder and harder not to touch her in a much more intimate way. He wanted to kiss her, to ravish her senses and relive the dreams that tormented his sleeping hours.

"Do you want to take a nap or anything before dinner?"

She blinked and then looked away. "I'd like to take a shower."

"Okay." He dropped his hand from her shoulder and went to put her stuff on the wooden chest at the end of the bed. "The water in the taps has gone through a distillery, so it's safe to drink or brush your teeth."

"That's good to know."

"Are you feeling all right?" Reluctant to leave, he looked for any excuse to stay.

"I'm not queasy anymore. Maybe the jog earlier calmed my stomach."

"It was more like a dash." He still had not recovered from the sight of his pregnant wife sprinting away from him. "I didn't mean to make you run."

"It wasn't your fault." Biting her lip, she looked at him with an appeal he did not know how to answer. "I overreacted to the reminder that I'd been a sober fool while you'd just been a drunk one."

So, that was what had upset her so much.

"I don't think you were a fool. I think you showed a lot of courage, then and now."

When she started shaking her head, he planted his hands on both of her shoulders and pulled her to him. "Shh. You took a chance on me, on what I promised you, and then you took a chance on coming down here. I'm not great on taking chances like that. I'll go into hostile territory to mine, but emotional commitment scares the hell out of me."

Her emerald green eyes widened.

"Fayre, I don't understand what's happening between us, but I know I can't let you go. I dream about you every night. We make love over and over again in my imagination. I couldn't see your face, and that drove me insane. I would have come looking when I got a break down here."

She shook her head again, her mouth opening, but no sound coming out.

"I don't expect you to believe me right off, but I do expect to convince you."

He tipped her hat off her head, remembering how the bill had jabbed his face when he'd kissed her earlier. She hadn't noticed, but he'd been forced to change his angle, and he didn't want anything in the way this time.

"Are you going to kiss me again?"

"Will it make you mad if I do?"

"I'll probably end up in bed with you, and then I'll feel stupid all over again."

She hadn't said she'd be angry with him, so he started to lower his head. "You don't need to feel stupid. I won't seduce you right now."

She licked her lips, and his heartbeat started pounding against his rib cage. "Promise?"

He'd promise her anything if she would just let him kiss her. "Yes."

"Then kiss me, Colton. Please."

He let his head lower the remaining inches until their mouths met, but he didn't take her lips hostage like a marauding Viking this time.

He wanted to savor her taste, the feel of her soft lips, her scent that was so different from his own.

Her lips parted on a gentle sigh, and he sent his tongue into her mouth on a slow, lazy glide.

She moaned softly, her hands coming up to grip his shirt in two tight fists. He cuddled her into his body, wrapping her up against him like the treasure she was.

He'd never enjoyed kissing a woman as much as he liked kissing Fayre. Except in his dreams, and now he knew they were about her, too.

Her soft breasts pressed against him, their nipples hardened into tight points that challenged his self-control.

"You're so sweet." He said the words into her mouth and then slanted his over hers again, preventing her from replying.

He kissed her for as long as he could without stripping her naked and taking her up against the wall.

He broke his mouth away and forced himself to step backward. "You'd better take your shower, angel."

She might not believe it, but she was the only angel he wanted.

She swayed when he let go of her, so he grabbed her shoulders again and led her to the bathroom. When she did nothing but stand there and continue to stare at him with that glazed look in her eyes, he smiled.

He affected her and he liked it.

"Do you need some help getting undressed?"

"Maybe."

Shock sent his heart into overdrive, but he wasn't giving her a chance to change her mind. Tugging her T-shirt off over her head, he sucked in air when her breasts held in by only a silky white bra came into view.

She was beautifully made, his showgirl wife.

He didn't immediately remove her bra, but unbuttoned her crop pants and pushed them down her thighs. Bending down, he slipped her sandals off, leaving her in a white satin G-string and matching bra. Because he was there and her body was so close, he leaned forward and inhaled the scent that made her all woman.

"Colton?"

He pressed his lips against the small white triangle of silk and kissed her there with something that felt like reverence. This woman was *his*.

Standing up, he gave himself the pleasure of simply staring at the view before him. Her hard nipples were visible behind the almost transparent satin of her bra, and the G-string left the long line of her sexy legs unbroken but for a tiny tantalizing ribbon. She shifted her feet, her thighs parting just a little, and he got a glimpse of chestnut curls, a shade darker than the hair on her head.

His heart about stopped and then tried to pound out of his chest. "You are the most beautiful woman I have ever seen."

Her soft green eyes shimmered with now familiar vulnerability. "Not as beautiful as Candy."

He was getting damn tired of her throwing the other woman in his face. "Way more beautiful than Candy."

"How would you know?"

"I remember her, and she has nothing on you. Angel, you just don't get it, but seeing you almost naked is like getting a sucker punch to the gut. I watched Candy dance all night and didn't even get a full boner."

Chapter Seven

"That's not true. You were . . ." Incredibly, she blushed. "You were fully erect when you came backstage and saw me."

"*When I saw you.*" Did she get the emphasis? "I saw you for what, five seconds, and went hard like a cannon ready to shoot." A lot like he felt right now. Only today, the fuse was lit, and the cannon was loaded.

Preventing it from going off was going to take a lot of self-discipline he wasn't positive he had.

"How do you know? You don't remember."

"Because that's exactly how I responded to you walking into the bar today. I figure drunk or sober, my reaction is going to be pretty much the same."

Her mouth opened and then snapped shut.

He nodded. "That's right. *You* are the woman I want."

He reached around her and turned on the water in the shower, deliberately letting his body rub against her almost naked one. She made a soft sound, but did not try to push him away. In fact, she swayed toward him infinitesimally, almost as if it had been an involuntary reaction. He took a lot longer than necessary adjusting the temperature of the water.

When he leaned back, her glazed look had returned.

He smiled again and slowly undid the clasp on the front of

her bra. He could feel the wild beat of her heart against the back of his hand. Keeping her gaze locked with his, he peeled the fabric back millimeter by millimeter. Her lips parted, and her breath panted out in short gasps as the backs of his fingers brushed the now exposed flesh of her breasts. Her beaded nipples had turned dark pink with engorged blood.

He put a palm against each one and rotated his hands until she was swaying again. "Do you like that?"

"Mmmm . . ."

He squeezed each creamy mound, and she arched against his hands, silently begging for more. Giving it to her was at the top of his list of priorities. He fondled her breasts until her head fell back, her eyes closed and her mouth opened on a silent, continuous moan.

Sliding one hand around her back and down to her buttocks, he lowered his mouth to claim hers again.

A man could get drunk on such sweetness.

He slipped his finger between her cheeks and then lower until he could feel the humid silkiness of her arousal.

He let his fingertip dip inside, and she went wild, arching into his body, thrusting her tongue into his mouth and locking her nails into his shoulders.

She taunted his tongue into sparring with hers in a mating dance that had him shaking with need in no time at all. He broke away from her and started stripping off his clothes.

When he was naked, she looked at him with an indecipherable expression in her eyes. "You are the sexiest man I have ever seen."

She said it with such seriousness that he didn't even try to shrug it off.

"Thank you."

He pushed her G-string down her legs and off. "Ready for your shower?"

"Yes."

He propelled her into the cubicle, and then he followed,

not even trying to keep their bodies separated in the small space. He'd promised not to seduce her, but he hadn't promised not to give her pleasure.

He planned to give her lots of pleasure.

He started by washing her hair, massaging her scalp with rhythmic motions that made her groan. "That feels so good."

"Does it?"

"You're pretty talented with stuff like this for a man who doesn't date much."

Had he told her that? He supposed he had. It seems he'd told her all his secrets when he was drunk, and that was bothering him less and less.

"With you, honey, it's pretty much instinct."

She laughed and dropped her head back against his chest. "Right."

How could he explain? He wanted to make her feel good; he would do anything to give her pleasure. It didn't have anything to do with what he'd done to other women in the past. "What we have is unique."

It was the best he could do. He didn't want her arguing with him, or questioning something he himself did not understand, so he turned her around and rinsed all the suds from her long hair. He liked this position. It put her breasts right up against him, but it was also too damn dangerous if he wanted to keep his promise.

When he was done rinsing her hair, he guided her around again, so she was facing away from him, and started soaping her body. Beginning at her neck and working his way downward, he paid special attention to her breasts and those wonderful turgid nipples.

"You're driving me crazy, Colton . . ." His name faded to a snaking moan as he pinched both nipples lightly and then pulled.

Licking the water from her ear, he whispered, "I want you *insane* with pleasure."

She shivered and reached behind her to touch him. Pressed as close as they were, she could only touch his hips. Thankfully. He couldn't have kept his cool if she'd gotten her hands on his throbbing erection.

"I want to touch you."

"Later. Right now is for you."

She shook her head, the wet mass of her hair rubbing against his chest and exciting him in a way he was damn sure she didn't intend or realize. He let go of her nipples, and she cried out in protest.

It was the sweetest kind of music, and he readjusted his hold on her. With one hand pressed against her stomach, he dropped the other one to her mound. He played with the silky curls there, loving the perfectly groomed tuft. Her skin was so smooth to either side, he was sure she waxed. She'd have to in order to wear the costume he'd seen on the floor of his hotel room six weeks ago.

He'd give pretty much anything to see it *on her*.

Gently separating the folds of her lips, he pressed a finger down over her swollen clitoris, and her body jerked. He brushed the small bud once, twice, three times.

She moaned and went lax against him, spreading her legs to rest against his, giving him nonverbal permission to do whatever he wanted.

Such trust was darn near enough to send him over the edge, but that was not the plan for right now.

"You're so sexy."

He rubbed the swollen and sensitive flesh lightly, swirling his finger in a circle, then up and down motion until she was trembling and rubbing her bottom against him in blatant invitation.

Tempted beyond reason to take her this way, to accept the invitation, he forced himself to keep his hard cock pressed against her back. He wasn't going to let her feel stupid again.

He was going to prove to her that he could give as well as take and that he wasn't just interested in an easy score.

He wanted a lot more.

He wanted all of her.

For a lifetime.

Pleasure detonated inside of Fayre with the power of a TNT blast. Her entire body bowed, every muscle in rigor as she experienced an explosive climax.

He didn't stop touching her, but used his fingers to ride out her orgasm until she was crying, begging him to stop.

"It's too much."

"No, angel, it's not enough."

Echoes of things he had said before somehow made them real again, taking away the sting of thinking they'd all been so much baloney, because he was saying them now, sober and aware.

He did pull back a little, just brushing her throbbing lips and not her clitoris, while he whispered stuff in her ear.

Things about what he wanted to do to her, what he wanted her to do to him, making her hot and trembly all over again.

And he knew it.

He started touching her more intimately, dipping inside her body with his big finger and using the heel of his hand to upbraid the engorged tissues around her sweet spot. With each successive stroke, the pleasure built all over again until she cried out and came once more, this time going completely limp against him, her limbs unable to support her even leaning against his hard thighs.

He held her up with one big hand and used the other to finish washing her. Then he picked her up and lifted her out of the shower. Drying her off had to be a challenge for him because she couldn't seem to make any of her muscles obey her so she could help.

He didn't complain, though.

He smiled. "You're so beautiful, Fayre."

Tears filled her eyes, and she choked out, "Thank you."

He kissed away the wetness under her eyelids and then kissed her mouth. "Thank you," he whispered against her lips.

"For what?"

He set her on a small bench situated against the wall beside the shower and then dried himself with the same towel he'd used on her.

It seemed like such an intimate thing to do, and she felt a warm tingling low in her belly.

"For letting me touch you."

It took her a second to figure out what he meant. Her mind was muzzy from fatigue and pleasure.

"I didn't do anything for you." The evidence was bobbing in front of him in semierect arousal.

"You didn't feel the extra wetness on your back? I came the second time you did."

So that was why he wasn't sporting a raging hard-on. She remembered his phenomenal stamina and rejuvenating powers from their wedding night. Given the slightest provocation, he could be capable of making love to her in less than five minutes.

"You didn't seduce me." They'd made a kind of love, but he'd known and *cared* that she wasn't prepared for full intercourse.

"I promised."

"And you keep your promises?"

"Yes." He picked her up again and carried her into the bedroom. "You have reason to doubt it, but when I make a promise, I keep it."

He tucked her into her bed and then turned to go, his naked body gleaming in the orange glow from the sunset outside.

"Colton."

He stopped at the door. "Yeah?"

"I'm not hungry right now."

"I figured that. You can take a nap. You look wiped."

She smiled. "From sexy to wiped. That's a pretty big come-down."

His laughter warmed something deep inside her. "You're sexy no matter how tired you are, Fayre."

"Are you hungry?"

He turned completely around. "What are you asking?"

"I want you to hold me." She felt stupid as soon as she said it, but the pathetic truth was out. She wanted to lean on his strength and draw from it for a little while.

"I'd like that. A lot." He came back to her, pulling the covers out to climb in beside her.

She snuggled into the warm hardness of his body. "Thank you."

"The pleasure is mine. I promise you."

She didn't reply as her brain shut down in sleep.

The scent of spicy Mexican food drew Fayre from sleep. Her hand immediately went in search of Colton, but the bed beside her was empty. She kept her eyes tightly shut. This was exactly how she'd woken the day after her wedding, and it was not a good feeling. She'd reached for her new husband, and he hadn't been there.

She'd opened her eyes, expecting to see him somewhere in the hotel room, only to see evidence of his departure.

The spicy smells teasing her into further wakefulness told her she was not alone in the house, but still she did not want to open her eyes.

Then a warm hand slid against hers, interlocking their fingers. "Dinner's ready, Fayre. Do you want me to bring it in here, or would you rather eat at the table?"

She turned her head toward the sound of his voice, letting her eyes open. He was kneeling beside the bed, one hand and arm under the covers with her, the other reaching for her.

He brushed her thick and tangled hair away from her face.

244 / *Lucy Monroe*

"I'm sorry I wasn't here when you woke up, but I was worried about you not eating for so long. Soda crackers aren't exactly a healthy meal."

He knew that it bothered her to wake up alone and again . . . he cared.

She smiled, feeling warm and safe and hungry. "I'm starving, but I'd rather eat at the table."

"Okay. You probably want to put clothes on, don't you?"

She noticed that he was wearing a pair of brief shorts, but nothing else. She liked having his muscular, big body on display. "I'll just put on a wrap."

"Thank you." He said it as though she was doing him a favor.

In a way, she was. He'd asked her if she wanted to put clothes on with the same attitude he'd approached her the night they got married. Sort of diffident, definitely horny, and as if he'd give just about anything to see her naked.

Which had been pretty funny as her dancer's costume had covered only slightly more than her panties and bra.

He stood up, and she slid out of the bed, feeling his hot gaze like a touch while she crossed the room to her suitcase, then flipped it open and pulled out a short Chinese silk wrap. The purple satin had been embroidered with golden roses along the hem and a dragon in the same metallic thread on the back.

She slipped into it and tied the belt before turning around to face him.

His expression was so carnal, she shivered.

"You said you'd made dinner?"

He shook his head as if to clear it. "Yeah. It's warming on the stove."

She smiled, warmth curling up her insides. He was acting a lot like he had the night they met.

Then an awful suspicion made her frown. "You haven't been drinking while I was asleep, have you?"

He crossed over to her and kissed her right on her still frowning mouth. "Nothing but water. Come on, let's go eat dinner."

She followed him into the kitchen, the good smells getting stronger the closer they got.

He pulled a chair out for her at the wooden table under one of the windows. Darkness had fallen outside, but the gentle glow of the light hanging from the ceiling made it an appealing spot to eat.

She slid into the chair and watched in bemusement as he prepared two plates of enchiladas, rice and beans. There was a big bowl of fruit in the middle of the table already and a carafe filled with what looked like some kind of red juice.

He put one plate in front of her and sat down, setting the other one in front of him.

"Did you really cook this?" she asked.

"Yes. Moonbeam could subsist on salads and these amazing grainy breads. I needed more sustenance and started cooking at a pretty early age." He was so big, she could not imagine him living on such a limited vegetarian diet and had no problem imagining him stubbornly learning to cook. "I made my first lasagna when I was nine."

She took a bite of her enchilada and almost moaned her appreciation. Delicious. "I didn't learn to cook until I moved to Vegas when I was eighteen."

He poured her a glass of juice. "Why was that? Did your mom have a problem with kitchen territorialism?"

She laughed at the description but shook her head. "My mom abandoned me to foster care when I was eight years old. I don't remember living any place with a real kitchen before that, just a lot of seedy hotel rooms."

His hand stilled in the act of taking a bite. "Did you get adopted?"

"No. Mom didn't relinquish parental rights. She kept saying she was going to come back for me."

"But she never came back."

"She died when I was twelve. By then I had a major attitude problem with authority. No one wanted to adopt a hellion, and I was one."

"It must have been rough."

"Yeah, but something really good happened that year, too. I learned to dance. No matter where I went, what foster home I ended up in, I had my dancing. The state paid for my lessons, or got me into community programs. My social worker was a really decent lady. It wasn't her fault I was so hard to live with."

"I can't imagine you being hard to live with."

She laughed. "That's because you didn't know me then. I tell you what, I'm going to know every trick a sneaky teen can pull, because I pulled them."

His gaze dropped to her waistline. There was no evidence yet of the life growing there, but she felt as though he could see into her with X-ray vision to the little baby developing in her womb. "You're going to be a really good mom, Fayre."

"You think so?"

"I'm positive."

She didn't know what to say to that. If she asked why he was so sure, it might imply she didn't think she'd be a good mom, and she did. She would love her baby and would never abandon it. That meant a lot. She knew.

Turning her attention to her plate, she took a bite.

"So, you moved to Vegas and pursued a career in dancing."

He didn't say it with a sneer in his voice like a lot of people did. It was easy to equate the sexiness of her stage attire with a lax attitude regarding sexual intimacy, but that was as far from truth as you could get.

She'd made mistakes in her choices of men, but she'd never jumped into immediate sexual intimacy . . . except with Colton.

"It took a long time, but I eventually got a job dancing in the chorus."

"You can't dance pregnant."

"No."

He sat back in his chair. "Does that bother you?"

"Not really." She'd been ready to leave the competitive and sometimes cruel world of professional dance before she met Colton. Her pregnancy was just precipitating her plans. "I want to teach dancing. Maybe after the baby is born."

"I can set you up with a studio, but you don't have to go back to work right away if you don't want to."

He'd had the same generous attitude before. Whatever she wanted. "That's what you said the night we got married."

He looked at her with a question in his dark eyes.

"We talked about what we wanted out of a family, and I told you I dreamt of staying home with my babies, being a mom and loving them for a while without any distractions. You said you thought that would be great and that I could stay home as long as I wanted to. You'd never pressure me to take on a career or go back to the one I had."

That's when she'd said yes. Not because he was willing to support her financially, but because he had been so accepting of the woman behind the professional dancer façade. His generosity had touched her deeply inside, and that was when she'd known she was irrevocably in love with him.

"Sounds great."

"You're assuming we'll be together."

"We will be." Those brown eyes burned into her with such certainty she couldn't muster up an argument.

They finished their dinner, chatting about many of the same things they had discussed the night they met. And she learned something about Colton. He might have been drunk that night and acting out of character with her, but all the core beliefs he had espoused were the real thing.

She was falling in love all over again.

She stood up to clear the table, but he stood, too, and stayed her hand with a light grip on her wrist. "Fayre."

Just one word and it was all back. The sexual tension. The overwhelming masculine desire beating at her like a hot wind.

"I thought I'd do the dishes since you cooked."

"I have a better idea."

She made the mistake of looking into his eyes. The message there sent her body into immediate nuclear meltdown. "You didn't even remember me," she said in a desperate attempt to remind both of them why making love wasn't a good idea.

"I've spent every night for six weeks dreaming about you. When I touch you, it's like connecting with the rest of my body. You didn't make a mistake with me. We belong together, and one of these days you're going to believe that."

"You left."

"I was coming back."

"You forgot our marriage."

"So, let's get married again. I'll remember this one, I promise. You can wear a white Mexican dress with lots of lace, and I'll hold your hand in front of a priest in the oldest church for three hundred miles."

"You want to get married again?"

"Yes, but can we wait for Moonbeam to get down here? She can fly down tomorrow, and we can have the wedding the next day."

Her thoughts were swirling like a whirlpool after a storm. "You want your mom there?"

"I'd like my brothers, too, but I don't know if they can get here fast enough."

She squeezed her eyes shut to make sure she wasn't dreaming. It was just like the night six weeks ago, but this time he was sober, and she knew it. He meant it. He wanted to stay married to her. He wanted another wedding, one he could remember.

"A dress will sure cover a lot more than my original wedding outfit," she said, trying to lighten his intense regard with a joke.

"Maybe you can wear it on our honeymoon."

She couldn't answer because he'd given in to the living desire shimmering between the two of them and kissed her. Hard masculine lips cherished her mouth instead of devouring it, and any protest she would have made died unspoken.

She didn't want to fight him. She wanted to believe they could have a future together because the feelings he invoked in her were real and they were strong.

Still buzzing from the pleasure he'd given her earlier, her body reacted to his kiss like a power plant on overload, every nerve ending sparking with electric intensity. She needed body contact. *Now.*

Untying her robe with a jerk, she let the purple silk fall open. One step and her body was pressed against his, her breasts nestled against the hot, naked planes of his chest. It felt incredible, but it wasn't enough. She wanted to experience all of him against all of her.

With impatient movements, she pushed his shorts down and then had to put a brake on herself and pull the waistband out so she could free his impressive erection when it got caught on the fabric and he groaned.

She wanted it; she wanted him with a feral desire that came from deep inside her.

His entire body jerked when her hand closed possessively around the part of his body she wanted buried deep in her.

And still his lips cherished hers, his tongue brushing the seem of her lips with gentle insistence until she opened her mouth. She sucked on his tongue, kissing him with aggressive desire she'd only ever let loose with this man.

On a fundamental level she trusted him more than she'd ever trusted another human being in her life.

That trust had been betrayed, but he was intent on making up for it, and she was of a mind to let him. At least if it meant joining his body with hers right now.

She caressed his hard length, stroking up and down and gently cupping him at the base.

A shout erupted out of him that she swallowed into her mouth, taking the sound captive in her throat as if it belonged to her as much as he did.

And he did belong to her.

At least for right now.

Two big hands cupped her backside and lifted. She had to relinquish her hold on his hardness as he physically lifted her so she could straddle him. She locked her legs behind his back and moaned into *his* mouth as the broad tip of his penis pressed against the still swollen and already very wet flesh of her opening. He teased her, letting his head slide inside of her a little deeper with each thrust, but not giving her the deep penetration she craved.

She tried to press down, but his hold on her was too tight.

She ripped her mouth from his. "I want you inside me, Colton. All the way!"

But instead of lowering her body, he lifted her farther up until he barely maintained contact between their two sexes. Then she felt his mouth on one aching nipple.

He sucked gently and kissed her, laving her breast with his tongue, rubbing his stubble-roughened cheek against flesh already highly sensitized. "You've got the most beautiful breasts I've ever seen."

And to prove he meant what he said, he turned and gave her other swollen curve the same treatment, using his tongue and lips in ways that brought tears of frustration spilling out of her eyes.

It felt so good, but she wanted, needed, his complete possession.

"Please, Colt, don't make me wait!"

He went still. "You call me that in my dreams."

He really did remember her in his dreams. She'd called him Colt from almost the first, and he'd liked it. "This isn't a dream."

"No, it's not." He started moving, and then she felt a wall against her back.

With torturous slowness, he lowered her body until she had the same maddeningly shallow penetration he'd given her before.

Dark brown eyes caught hers. "You are mine."

"Yes."

His mouth came down on hers again with more passion than before, but no less care. It was all pleasure, and then he thrust up into her, seating himself completely in her body. She gasped at the full feeling, shocked anew by the length and breadth of his excited flesh.

It was too much, but she couldn't let him leave her.

He rocked his hips, thrusting inside her with short but powerful movements, caressing her insides, stretching her to a point that was just this side of pain, but was oh, so full of blissful gratification for her feminine flesh.

His kiss grew increasingly demanding until his tongue possessed her mouth with the same effectiveness of his erection in her body.

She dug her fingernails into his shoulders and tightened her legs around him, keeping him deep inside her as they moved together against the kitchen wall.

Feelings that were so much more than physical buffeted her heart and her body as pleasure spiraled a notch tighter with each movement of his big body against hers. Her muscles locked in preparation for climax. Incredibly, he swelled even more inside her as his body pounded against hers.

The pleasure burst and splintered inside her, so strong that she stopped breathing for several seconds, a soundless scream vibrating in her throat as her body bowed against his. His shout was loud and feral as he tore his head away from hers and climaxed with more power than anything she'd ever known.

"*Fayre.*" It was a rough shout of completion, of continued need, of absolute possession.

Her lungs expanded, and she cried out, "*Love me!*" as his powerful orgasm spilled her body over into a second one.

"Yes, angel." He hugged her tightly to him, continuing his thrusting, both their bodies vibrating with their mutual pleasure. "*Yes.*"

They both shuddered with the aftershocks as oversensitive flesh rubbed against oversensitive flesh until finally, he went completely still against her. Of their own volition, her ankles unlocked, and her legs dropped down so that she was held up and pinned against the wall by his body's intimate connection with hers only.

"We need a bed."

"The dishes . . ." A dumb thing to remember after such incredible pleasure.

"Can wait."

Placing a hand under each armpit, he lifted her and stepped backward. Then he slowly lowered her to a standing position.

"How do you have the energy to do that?" She was in good physical shape, but after what they'd just shared, it was all she could do to lean against the wall and not fall on her fanny.

"I'll let you walk to bed." He said it like a concession, and she was unconvinced it had a thing to do with him not being able to lift her.

She smiled, though. He was such a wonderful man. He didn't want her to feel like a weakling. "Thank you."

He insisted on showering before sleep, and this time he let her wash him, too. He about deafened her with his response to soap lather on his nether regions. Afterward, he carried her to bed, and she teased him about being a caveman.

He made love to her with her hair wrapped around his fist Neanderthal fashion. He was careful not to pull it, but she experienced an extra level of excitement at his blatant male possessiveness, even if it was a joke.

He was still caressing her when she fell asleep, exhausted from a marathon of lovemaking she had no idea any man could sustain. Even him.

Colton woke up in the middle of the night with his wife nuzzled into his side and felt as though he'd made it to paradise. No longer taunted by dreams, but satisfied beyond belief by reality, his face split in an uncharacteristic grin in the darkness.

She was his now.

He was sure of it.

They'd made love over and over again the night before until he'd finally tired the little thing out.

She'd fallen asleep as her body convulsed in something like her tenth orgasm. Hell, it could have been more.

Not that it mattered. The only thing he cared about was whether or not she believed she could trust him.

It would help when she woke up and he was still there. Not like six weeks ago or even the day before when he'd left her bed to make her dinner. He'd watched her waken, thinking she would open her eyes and look at him, only to see her hand go questing and come up empty.

Then her face had contorted, and he knew she was remembering, so he'd rushed over to find that questing hand and let her know he would always be at the other end of it from now on. He was determined to be next to her when she woke up this morning, but he had a couple of things to do first.

She was sleeping so soundly and had been so exhausted when she had fallen asleep, he figured he had at least a few hours before she woke up.

* * *

This time when she awoke, the only thing Fayre could smell was the masculine, earthy scent of the man beside her. Her hand had not even moved an inch before it encountered warm male flesh. Opening her eyes, she smiled like she had not smiled in weeks.

He was awake already, watching her, his own lips curved in a grin. "Hi."

"Good morning, Colt."

"You slept a long time. It's no longer morning."

The lack of direct sunlight in the room gave a deceptive impression that it could be early morning, but one quick peek at the alarm clock proved him right. "It's almost one o'clock!"

"Yes."

She bit her bottom lip. "I guess you woke up a long time ago?"

He reached out and brushed his finger along her lip and then tucked her hair back behind her ear. "You could say that."

"But you stayed with me."

"I didn't want you to wake up alone."

"Which is sweet, if a bit ridiculous. He wouldn't let us wake you up either."

At the sound of a feminine voice coming from the doorway, Fayre craned her neck to see who was talking.

"Hello, Fayre. I'm Moonbeam."

Her name fit her extremely well. The woman standing on the other side of the room had hair the color of a moonbeam. Her tiny body and pixieish face also seemed more ethereal than human, and Fayre could completely understand why Colton described her as a flower child.

Her clothes weren't tie-dyed, but the flowy silk top and matching pants had been batiked with vibrant shades.

Fayre grabbed the sheet and pulled it to her chin. "Nice to meet you."

Colton sat up, apparently totally unconcerned about his wide expanse of naked chest and stomach. Of course, the woman was his mother.

"Moonbeam, I asked you to wait until I brought Fayre out to meet you."

The older woman put one hand on her hip, looking an awful lot like a mother despite her startling appearance. "You didn't ask, you told. Which is impolite as I'm your mother. Your brothers are eager to meet your wife, too . . . or should I say fiancée? This whole getting married twice idea is lovely, but a little confusing."

Fayre stared up at Colton, feeling very much as if she'd been hit by a truck. "Your brothers are here, too? You told them about our wedding?"

What must they think? Colton had not once accused her of being a gold digger who had taken advantage of his inebriated state, but his family wouldn't be as trusting. They didn't know her, and she'd had too much experience with being the recipient of negative assumptions to believe now would be any different.

"How did they get here so fast?"

"Yes. Yes and they flew on Rand's private jet. I wouldn't mind having one of those."

"But how . . ."

"Colton called everyone in the middle of the night last night to tell us the news and ask us to come," Moonbeam answered for her son.

"Is she awake?" This time it was a masculine voice.

Fayre dove under the covers. "Tell him to go away." Her hair was a disaster, and she was naked.

"She's awake, but I don't think she's coming out until you and Moonbeam leave."

Fayre nodded under the covers in agreement.

The man chuckled, and then another feminine voice intruded. "I want to meet her, too."

"Is that Fayre?" yet another woman asked.

"Well, if it's a party, why wasn't I invited?" The voice sounded so much like Colt that if he hadn't been right next to her, she would have wondered if it was him.

Was it Carter or Rand? She remembered their names, but Colt had never said anything about one of them sounding just like him. Maybe the men didn't notice. She bet her sister-in-law did.

"It's not a party." Colton was laughing, so the words came out choked.

Fayre kicked him under the blanket.

He said a not very nice word.

"Come along. I'll see about making lunch." Moonbeam's voice left no room for opposition.

"I want more than salad," Colton warned.

"I'll help her." The offer came from one of Colton's brothers, not the other women.

It was silent for several seconds before Colton tugged at the sheet and light blanket she'd burrowed under. "They're gone. You can come out."

She dropped the blankets and sucked in a big breath of air, glaring at her husband the whole time. "If your whole family is here, what are you doing in bed with me?"

"I didn't want you to wake up alone."

"That's nice, but don't you think bringing your mom, brothers and sisters-in-law in on it was overdoing it a tad?"

His smile was all rascal. "I didn't put them in bed with us, did I?"

"They probably think I'm some bimbo who tricked you into marriage when you were drunk."

"Why would they think that?"

"You were drunk when we got married."

"So? Moonbeam thinks getting drunk that night was the smartest thing I've ever done and leaving without talking to you was the dumbest."

"You told her all of it?" Fayre threw the covers back over her head. "She's going to hate me."

Instead of pulling the covers off of her, Colton tunneled under them. "She's going to love you."

"She'll think I got pregnant to trap you into marriage."

Colton kissed her, and Fayre forgot everything but the sensation of having him so close.

When he lifted his head, the blankets slid down to leave them both exposed. "Fayre, my family is happy for us. Okay?"

"How can they be? You married a showgirl! I remember what you told me about your brothers. They're both rich. They attend charity balls and drive sports cars that cost more than some people's houses. Rand is married to a woman who is a descendant of the founding family in their hometown. She owns this island. The only thing I own of any value is my car. Don't you see the difference?"

Colton's eyes were warm and incredibly tender. "All I see is a woman I would give my life for."

Tears filled her eyes, and she punched his shoulder. "Don't say things like that."

"Why not? It's true. I don't care about money or who your grandparents were. I only care that when I'm with you, I don't feel like the secret bastard son of Hoyt Sloane. I feel like a man worthy of an amazing woman's love and courage."

She bit her lip, trying to stop its trembling, but nothing could stop the tears spilling over from her eyes. "I d-do l-love you."

His mouth came down again, and he kissed away the tremble and the tears.

Then he slid off of her and onto the floor beside the bed.

Leaning over, he grabbed something off the nightstand and then faced her. "I don't remember asking you to marry me, and I want that memory to share with our children."

She sat up and clutched the sheet in her hands, not bothering to cover her body. It belonged to him, and his family had closed the door when they left.

It was just her and Colton.

"You got down on your knees in the middle of the restaurant."

He smiled. "I like this better." And he was looking at her, all of her, but not with lust, with awe.

Frissons of joy went all through her.

He took her left hand and rubbed the back of it with his thumb. "I love you, Fayre, will you marry me?"

She was too choked up to reply, but she nodded until it felt like her head would pop off.

Then she felt a ring sliding onto her finger, and she looked down. A big square-cut emerald glittered up at her.

"We'll both wear rings after the ceremony at the Mexican church." He said it like a vow.

She swallowed.

"I love you, Colt. I don't understand how I could love you so much so fast, but I do."

"I know, Fayre. I feel the same way. I fell in love with you on sight six weeks ago, and I did it again yesterday. Please don't ever make me live without you."

She shook her head until he stopped the movement with another kiss.

Far from thinking the worst of her, Colton's family embraced Fayre from the moment she made her first nervous entry into the kitchen. His brother Carter had made lunch as her new sister-in-law Daisy had been quick to point out. She was obviously totally besotted, and Fayre thought that was sweet. Rand and Phoebe were too busy canoodling in a chair by the table for them to be of any help at all with the meal, but no one else seemed to mind.

No one made her feel uncomfortable, least of all Colt's mother. Fayre saw a lot of the person he had been while he was inebriated in his mother and hoped that over time, he would show more of that playful side without the inducement of alcohol.

But he was anything but playful during their wedding ceremony the next day. As promised, he'd bought her a white Mexican dress with lots and lots of handmade lace. Moonbeam had lamented the lack of color, but agreed with Colton that Fayre looked like an *angel* in it.

Her gaze locked with his while she repeated her marriage vows, and he never once broke eye contact when he said his back.

Then he kissed her. It was a lot more flammable than she was expecting in front of his family and the priest, so she was high in his arms and being carried from the church before she realized the ceremony was over.

He broke the kiss as they stepped out into the bright sunshine. "You're mine, Fayre. Now and forever."

She'd wanted to hear those words her entire life, and they wrapped themselves around her heart like a protective shield she could always hide behind. She belonged to someone.

"And you're mine."

He nodded and kissed her again.

His brothers and their wives joined Fayre and Colton on the steps.

Moonbeam smiled at them all, her expression turning fey. "It was each of your destinies to break the cycle of pain from the past, and you've done it."

Colton looked down at Fayre. "If that's true, then I've got my destiny in my arms."

She didn't want to cry again, so she grinned instead. "Do you notice you're carrying me again? Moonbeam, you've raised a real unreconstructed man here, and I'm wondering how that happened when you're so progressive in your thinking."

Colton pretended to drop her and then threw back his head and laughed out loud when she screamed.

She knew she would love this man until the day she died, and he would love her.

It was their destiny.